GROWING ATTRACTION

GROWING ATTRACTION

•

Lynn M. Turner

AVALON BOOKS
NEW YORK

PRINTED IN THE UNITED STATES OF AMERICA
ON ACID-FREE PAPER
BY HADDON CRAFTSMEN, BLOOMSBURG, PENNSYLVANIA

To the beautiful Annapolis Valley

Chapter One

Anna MacFrail felt something was wrong the moment she opened her kitchen door. She stood on the back porch with her hands braced on the railing, her eyes scouring the property. The farmhouse sat at the foot of a slope so she could see most of the back acres and the lines of succulent young plants growing there. She turned left toward the huge barn and had to shade her eyes from the early morning sun glaring off its expanse of white wall. Everything looked normal.

Her first thought was the chickens. She could hear them clucking and complaining as they did every morning, but that didn't mean anything. A couple of months earlier a dog had burrowed

1

under the fencing of one of the runs and ravaged a half-dozen hens before she'd been able to get the little critter under control. Once the confusion died down, the hens acted as if nothing had happened, so their lack of commotion this morning didn't necessarily mean anything.

She walked down the steps and across the lawn past the blooming lilacs. Even their sweet smell seemed strange, different. When she rounded the end of the barn a stiff breeze made her pull up the zipper on her hooded sweatshirt. The chickens saw her and cranked the volume. *Gwaaaa! Gwaaa! Come now! Feed us! Now! Feed us!*

Almost eight dozen hens, healthy Rhode Island Reds with shiny brown feathers and bright red combs, pushed and shoved to get a better look at her, the source of food.

The previous year, Anna had built six runs parallel to one another like the tines on a fork, all entering a common area in the basement of the barn. She had designed it so that every few weeks, when the ground where the chickens foraged started to look too packed down, she could move the hens to the grassy area in the middle simply by closing off the ends. That way they could eat fresh grass without being exposed to the perils of the wild.

She ignored the noise and strode along

searching for a break in the fence. Everything looked sound. And so it should, she thought, since she'd just buried the wires another foot deeper. Still, the uneasy feeling crawled up her spine.

Other than a few hired laborers during harvest, Anna ran this small farm by herself. She didn't have time to worry about gut feelings.

"Okay, girls, I'm coming."

The hens tripped all over themselves trying to get back inside the barn. They weren't starving. There was always some feed in the bottom of their troughs, but they didn't like the dusty ends. The lower level of the barn had been divided into two sections: one for the chickens, the other for storage. Anna left the wide doors open behind her, then moved along scooping out feed and dropping it in the chutes that emptied into the trough on the chicken's side. As the hens ate, they quieted. She could hear the dull thud of their beaks hitting the food. Over that sound came the throaty grind of a tractor running nearby. She wondered about that, but before going to investigate, she hosed out the water trenches and topped up the reservoirs. She'd come back later and collect the morning's eggs.

Ricky, the cat who had been with her since she bought the farm, slipped in and out between Anna's feet. She scooped the soft bundle into her arms and scratched it under the chin. Ricky purred and nuzzled closer.

"What do you want? Huh?" Anna would have loved to get a string and trail it along the ground for the playful cat, but didn't have the time. With a sigh, she released her.

The low slanting sun streamed in the eastern windows, lighting up the swirling dust from the hay and feed. It was an old barn with thick, hand-hewn beams, and wide plank walls. On this side, the ground was packed red dirt. The chicken's side was strewn with wood chips.

Back outside, Anna pulled the peak of her baseball cap further down to shade her eyes and undid the top button of her sweater. It was going to be a glorious June day, the kind of day she would dream about in the depth of winter when the snow blanketed everything and the land-scape looked starkly black and white.

The tractor sound came from the far side of the grape trellises, beyond a copse of trees. Anna snapped off a sprig of lemon thyme and crushed it under her nose as she passed the young vines. They'd reached the first rung of the trellis and would soon need to be pruned and trained. She was thinking about how to fit that chore into her schedule when she rounded the rise.

On the west side, Anna's farm abutted a dirt

road. The nearby fields were owned by the VanOrthrums, an old Valley family who had worked the same land for generations, although they now lived twenty minutes down the road in the farming community of Suffenbrook. This year, these fields were planted in carrots, so Anna expected to see someone working up the soil between the rows. What she saw instead had her gasping with disbelief. A tractor pulled a red tank spewing white liquid. The dirt road was dark with moisture because the wind was lifting the spray and carrying it right over to her fields.

She broke into a run. "Stop! What are you spraying? Stop!"

The tractor continued its relentless roll up the hill. Anna caught a whiff of the noxious herbicide and her heart clenched. Broad-leaf killer. She sprinted up the dirt rise yelling at the top of her lungs. Finally the driver caught sight of her and pulled to a stop. The tractor kept running, but the high-pitched buzz of the sprayer whined down.

Anna's long, jean-clad legs leapfrogged over rows of fuzzy new carrot plants. When she neared the tractor the door opened, and a man she'd never seen before looked out at her. He wore a grimy baseball cap backwards, and dirty overalls that strained across his ample belly.

"Something wrong?" he asked.

"Your spray," Anna said, almost yelling to be heard above the engine, "it's drifting to my . . . my cole crops."

He stood and looked east. Then he pulled off his cap and ran his fingers through his thin, oily hair. "Lord love us, I started before sunrise. Didn't see that."

She glanced at her young cabbage transplants and almost cried. She'd coaxed every one of them from seed in her greenhouse and planted them by hand. Broad-leaf killer was well named; it killed everything it touched that had a broad leaf. Carrots and grain were left unharmed, but her poor transplants were doomed. "I'm ruined."

"Now Miss," he said in a kindly voice, "can't be but five rows hit."

"Five rows for how long? Must be two acres."

"That's right. Only two acres. Crop insurance'll cover that."

Two acres might be nothing to him, but she only worked twenty. "It's not just that. I'm organic. You just sprayed a chemical on my land."

"Aw, I'm sorry about that. Listen, nobody needs to know about this, eh? We'll get the boss to cover—"

"What do you mean *nobody needs to know*," she demanded, infuriated. "The plants are dead now, or soon will be. And even if they weren't—what are you doing spraying on a windy day anyway?"

"Just doing what I'm told. You're really over-reacting."

"Orsen VanOrthrum told you to spray here? I don't believe it." He was one of the few people in the farming community who was friendly with Anna.

"Not Orsen. Del."

"Del?"

"His son. Orsen retired."

She didn't believe this either. Orsen wouldn't retire without telling her. Unless something had happened to him in the few weeks since she'd last seen him. She hoped not; Orsen was such a nice person.

The smell of the herbicide was making her stomach turn. "And where is this Del right now?"

"Back at the house, I guess."

"Turn that thing off and come with me."

"Huh?"

"We'll go see him right now."

"Listen lady, I'm sorry about your field and all, but I'm not going nowheres. I've got to finish this here job."

Anna pried her fists open and took three calming breaths. "You're new at farm work, aren't you?"

"No I am not. I worked at the Lighthorn Farms for six years."

Lighthorn Farms grew tobacco and rotated it with strawberries, so this man had little experience with mixed crops. Still . . . "Then you should know better than to spray into the wind."

"Hey! I leave the thinking up to the owner. I do what I'm told."

"What you've been told is wrong! Please! Let's go see Del VanOrthrum."

He took another look at the damp cabbage field then turned back to her. "I'll tell you what. You go talk to the boss. I'll do some maintenance on this here rig and then I'll have a coffee break. If you're not back when I'm done, I'll start up again."

"Not here. Please don't spray here. Once the field's contaminated, I can't claim organic status."

"Oh for Pete's sake. I'll move over to the other side." He slammed the cab door.

Anna jogged back down the dirt road and around to the front of the barn where she parked her truck. No one locked their doors in Havenville, and she kept an extra key under the mat, so she was out on the road in a matter of seconds. With one hand on the wheel, she rolled down her window. The smell of the herbicide stuck to her clothes and clung to her nostrils.

Oh, but this was a disaster. In order to be certified organic she had to prove that nothing inorganic had been used on the field within three years of harvest. People who bought her produce wanted to be confident that they weren't eating any insecticides, herbicides, fungicides, or chemical fertilizers. Three years earlier Olsen VanOrthrum agreed to keep sprays away from her land in return for her providing his family with organic eggs. Apparently his son was unaware, or didn't care, about the arrangement.

The VanOrthrums lived in a square three-story house with white siding and black shutters. It stood alone on a rise of land, cupped by various barns and outbuildings, and facing a slope of still-green grain. As Anna drove up the smooth driveway she wracked her brain trying to remember if she'd ever met this Del Van-Orthrum. She had a vague memory of Orsen talking about him—complaining really—but couldn't remember the exact conversation. It had something to do with Del getting over-educated and spending his days working in-doors.

She pulled behind the house and left the truck by the back door. A great fluffy dog bounded toward her, barking and waving its tail. She tried to ignore it, but the dog rammed her in the thigh.

"Yes, dog, yes. Aren't you nice," she mumbled, rubbing its head. "I don't have time to get to know you now." She gently pushed it on the shoulder, then limped up to the kitchen door and rapped hard. After a couple of seconds, she walked backward away from the door and yelled, "Hello? Anyone home? Hello?"

The kitchen curtains flipped aside to reveal a man's face: dark hair all askew, a couple of day's worth of beard growth, startlingly intense eyes. The curtain dropped again. Anna's own reflection stared back at her; a delicate face with large eyes bracketed by long lashes and prominent cheekbones. A moment later she heard a lock turning. The door opened about ten inches, and the man peered out.

"What?" He snarled.

Anna was so taken aback, first by the door being locked—no one locked their doors in these parts—and then by his rudeness, that she stared at him a moment too long. He started to close the door again with a snarl.

"We don't want any."

"Excuse me?" Anna gasped. The thought of that worker spraying back at her own farm gave her the extra oomph to grab the edge of the door so he couldn't shut it without crushing her fingers. "Is Orsen here? I need to talk to him."

"Nope. He'll be gone all summer." The door started to close again.

"Are you Del VanOrthrum?"

The man's face contorted in a massive yawn. The motion brought his hand to his mouth so Anna was able to shove the door open all the way. He wore a rumpled oxford shirt and buff-colored trousers. She wanted to be assertive, and knew she should look him in the eye, but for some reason she found herself studying his feet instead. They were bare, and black hair curled on his tanned toes.

"Yeah," he finally said with a nod. "Sorry, I'm lousy at waking up."

She'd done an hour's worth of chores already and he was just waking up? "My name is Anna MacFrail," she started. "Did Orsen leave any instructions about the land next to mine? My farm down in Havenville?"

"Don't think so," he said. "Why?"

"You sent a man down to spray the carrots. Orsen wouldn't have wanted you to do that. You see, I'm an organic farmer."

"So?"

He turned around and started down the hall. She felt compelled to follow.

"The spray, it's drifting across my field."

"What's he spraying?"

"Herbicide."

They reached a large, airy kitchen with huge picture windows, a table big enough to seat twelve, and a massive six-burner stove. He reached into a cupboard for a giant blue tin of coffee. "Want a cup of coffee?"

"I don't have time," she said, trying to keep the impatience from her voice. "Your employee said he'd resume spraying if I didn't come back in a couple of minutes."

"What's his name?"

"I don't know. I've never seen him before. Listen, if you'd just come with me, or follow me down in your car, you could talk to him."

"He must be one of the new guys."

"Yes! He's new. Come on."

"Don't get your knickers all in a twist," he said. "By the sound of it, the damage is done already. What do you have planted?"

She felt like grabbing his elbow. "I'm an organic farmer. He's making the land unusable! Where are your shoes?" She started back toward the hall to find them.

"If you'd bothered to get his name," Del said, "I would—"

"I don't need a lecture on manners," she interrupted, thoroughly peeved by his lackadaisical manner.

"—know which tractor he took so I could phone him," he finished.

Now she looked fully in his face. "You can phone him?"

"Of course. All the tractors have cell phones."

"He didn't tell me that. Please call him right now."

"It'll just take me a minute to remember who I sent down to Havenville. . . ." Del walked over to a desk strewn with papers, magazines, and envelopes. He shuffled through them a bit, then picked up the phone.

Anna sunk onto a kitchen chair. Now that she'd accomplished her objective and he was actually telling the laborer to stop the spraying and to bring the tractor back, she allowed herself to relax and really look at Del VanOrthrum. What she saw made her wish she was wearing something other than her dirty work jeans and baggy sweatshirt. He was a tall man, over six feet, with wide shoulders and a full chest, but without an ounce of extra fat. His dark hair curled a bit in the back, over the collar of his shirt. Either he was growing a beard or he hadn't shaved in a couple of days. When he finished on the phone he turned and looked at her with dark brown eyes hooded by thick brows. Oh my, his eyes were gorgeous.

"Doesn't sound like there's too much damage," he said. "What do you have planted?"

She cleared her throat. "Cole crops. Cabbage and broccoli."

"You'll have to replant. Shouldn't be a problem. It's early in the season yet."

His dismissive tone had her clenching her fists again. "Where am I going to get organic seedlings? And even if I could, the soil is contaminated now."

"Organic seedlings? That's taking things a bit far, isn't it?"

"No, it isn't. You have no idea what you've done to me, do you? I've been running in the red as it is, and now you've probably taken away any hope of me seeing a profit this year."

"You don't need to cry poor with me. I know what an acre of crops is worth."

He thought she was trying to con money out of him. She jumped to her feet. "I wouldn't be in this mess if you hadn't ordered that man to go out into the field in the dark while you slept the morning away."

He looked at her again with hooded brow. "Listen lady," he drawled, "why don't you tell your husband to give me a call. We'll work out a fair settlement between us men."

"I have a better idea, sonny boy," she said through gritted teeth. "Why don't you get your father to call me. If anyone knows what an acre of my land is worth, he does!"

As she marched down the hall to the back door, Del VanOrthrum sputtered a few words that could have been intended as an apology. She was too angry to give him another second of her time.

Chapter Two

Del VanOrthrum stood in the middle of his kitchen floor in his bare feet with his ears still ringing from the slam of the back door. Outside, a vehicle started up. He stepped over to the sink and peered out the window in time to see a rusty quarter-ton truck pulling out of the yard, black smoke spewing from its exhaust.

He hadn't handled that well. In fact, he couldn't even remember apologizing for contaminating that woman's field. He rubbed his face, trying to wake up. In the previous forty-eight hours he'd only slept—he glanced at the clock—two hours. And that pretty little woman woke him from what little there was of it.

He badly needed coffee. Where were the filters? At least the kitchen cupboards were stocked. Del suspected his sister had something to do with that since Orson, his father, had left in a rush.

He poured some cereal into a bowl, then grabbed the milk from the refrigerator. The milk didn't so much pour as plop from the container. He peered at the stale date printed on the side, then scraped the whole mess into the garbage.

A week earlier, when his dad had asked him to come home and run the farm, Del had felt nervous but fairly confident. The timing couldn't have been better, because it coincided with the end of the term at the college where he taught. He had a master's degree in business administration, which, he figured, set him in good stead, since the Agri-Food industry was big business. Plus, he'd worked on the farm as a kid, so he could tell the difference between a lettuce plant and a potato sprout.

Already he'd made a big mistake. Perhaps he'd underestimated the job.

Del sat down at the desk, looked up his grandmother's number in the address book, and programmed it into the speed dial. Then he placed the call to Holland. His father answered.

"Hi Pop. How's Nanny?"

"Ah, well, she's not too good. Physically

she's strong, but she didn't recognize me at first."

"I'm sorry, Pop. That must have been hard on you."

"It really threw me. They're trying some new kind of stuff that should clear up her mind some."

They talked a few minutes about the situation; what the doctors thought and what the options were. Then Orsen asked, "How's it going back there?"

Del tried to sound optimistic. "The crew came over last night and brought me up-to-date. They all knew what they were to do this morning before they left. And I hired that man we talked about to replace old Harry."

"You mean Stubby?"

"You don't call him that to his face, do you?"

"That's how he introduces himself. Stubby Smith. He working out good?"

"So far. Listen, Dad, I sent him, ah, Stubby, over to Havenville to do some weed control on the carrots."

"Mechanically, I hope?"

"Well, no."

"I told you. No spraying over there."

Del couldn't remember anything being said about Havenville during their rushed conversations. "I haven't been up to see the situation firsthand yet, but I guess we did over-spray a bit. I'll have a talk with the owner. Do you think he'll be reasonable about a settlement?"

Orsen chuckled. "You haven't met the owner yet?"

"Just the woman."

"That's the owner. Anna MacFrail. Ha! Now who's being sexist?"

For years Del had been calling his father old-fashioned and sexist. It seemed the roles had reversed. "She told me to ask you what the value of an acre of her land was worth." Orsen didn't respond so he prodded, "Any suggestions?"

"Well now," Orsen drawled, "I think you and Anna should settle that between the two of you."

"You know she's organic, eh?"

"Oh yeah," he responded, emphatically.

"And their produce brings in a higher dollar at the market, so I can work out the actual value of the crops, but she's got some kind of story about me ruining her land."

"I've bookmarked the Organic Certification Board on the computer. Why don't you learn a bit about that before you see her."

"Pop!" He laughed. "You're not thinking of going organic on me are you?"

"Not at our scale. Can't compete. Just think you should read up some."

"Yeah, okay." Del couldn't imagine when

he'd find the time. "So, what's she like? Is she going to be reasonable?"

"She's a good person. Had a hard go of it, but she tries her best. Don't let her hard exterior fool ya."

"What kind of 'hard go'?"

"Hey, I'm not gonna sit here and gossip with you from the other side of the Atlantic Ocean."

"Listen, Pop, you give Nanny a hug from me will you? And look after yourself."

"You too, Son. Let me know how it goes with Anna."

Del wondered why his father sounded more interested in what happened with Anna than what was going on with his farm. A few acres here and there, a thousand dollars here or there, didn't mean anything to the profitability of Suffenbrook Farm. With hundreds of acres of crops to look after, he couldn't waste time on a little organic farmer, even if she did have a pert nose and shimmering blue eyes that were as pretty as anything he'd ever seen.

Maybe he should pencil her name in the calendar around the end of August. Perhaps then he'd have time to waste on dating. Still, he couldn't afford to alienate the locals. He decided to pay her a quick visit.

Twenty minutes later, Del, showered and shaved and dressed in a clean pair of jeans, drove up the dirt road bordering the Van-Orthrum fields in Havenville. The smell of the herbicide still hovered in the air, but the ground had dried. By the next morning, Anna Mac-Frail's affected crops would be drooping and yellow right along with the broad-leaf weeds in the carrot field, but now they looked well-tended and clear of pests. He drove back down the road and parked next to her truck in front of the barn.

She had an attractive property. The story-and-a-half farmhouse itself was small and close to the road, but it had a tidy front yard, and big-leafed hosta grew thickly all around the stone foundation. The windows were tall with wavy old glass that was, on closer inspection, single paned. That had to be cold in the winter. The paint on the shingles needed touching up too.

When there wasn't any reply to his knocking, he followed the sound of clucking and found her in the basement of the barn.

Anna stood with her back to the door. She was tall and a bit on the thin side, but she filled her jeans out nicely. A long ponytail hung out from the opening at the back of her baseball cap. Even in the gloom of the basement, her hair gleamed a sun-bleached blond. She was washing eggs in a shallow enamel sink under water that gushed from a green hose she'd looped over a couple of spikes. She reached her left hand into a bucket, plucked out three eggs at once, rubbed them with a cloth under the spray, and set them in a rubber draining rack. Then she reached again.

"Hi there."

Anna swung around. One egg flew from her hand and smashed on the dirt floor. Without a word, she plucked the shells out of the mess and threw them in with the chickens.

"Ricky! Come!" There was a scuffling noise overhead and an orange cat came bounding down the rickety stairs. "Here." Anna poked a finger into the broken egg's yolk, and the cat sniffed daintily at it.

"Sorry," he said. "Didn't mean to startle you."

The cat turned up its nose at the egg, so Anna cupped her hands around the goop and dirt and washed it down the drain. She didn't say anything, just looked, stony-faced.

He nodded toward the running water. "That's a pretty low-tech system you've got going there."

"It does the trick."

"I would have thought you'd use bleach or something." He stepped closer and saw that her fingers were red. There was only one off-valve at the end of the hose; the water must have come directly from the cold well. "And worn rubber gloves."

Anna wiped her hands on the wrung-out rag and took a big breath before saying, "I'll clean them again with a biodegradable solution when I get them into the house. What can I do for you, Mr. VanOrthrum?"

"Call me Del, please. Mr. VanOrthrum is my father." He smiled, but inside he was cringing. Such a lame joke.

She walked out of the barn. "I'll show you where the spray reached."

"I've already been. Listen, I want to apologize for the mix-up. You see, I just got in last night and the men had been trying to do what needed to be done but a couple of them were new and I just thought I'd better give them some assignments, you know, before I hit the sack. Then I heard about all the problems with the generators in the cold storage and I was up all night and . . ." He ran out of steam when he saw the way she was looking at him—angry, skeptical, with out-and-out dislike. He felt a disappointment that seemed out of proportion to the situation, and told himself he was just tired.

"Did you talk to your father?"

They were out in the sun now, walking next to a maze built of chicken wire. "Yeah. He said I was to deal fairly with you."

One side of her lip rose in half a smile. "Your father is a decent man."

"Yes, he is."

"Is it true he retired?"

"No, he's just taking some time off to look after his mother."

Anna stopped and frowned. "Is she ill? She's in Holland, isn't she?"

He didn't want to talk about his Nanny with this woman. She'd think he was trying to get her sympathy and give him that look again. He reached into his jeans for his wallet. "I brought a check. What do you figure you'll be out because of all this?"

She crossed her arms. "I haven't had time to figure it yet."

"Want to do that now?"

"It's not a simple thing. I've got over ten acres of cole crops in."

"Yeah, but only the bit by the road is affected."

"I can't sell the unaffected produce as organic even if it is."

"Why not?"

"It's in the regulations."

He thought about that website his father wanted him to visit and decided to keep his mouth shut about organic farming until he knew what he was talking about.

A car horn tooted. Without a word, Anna strode off to the corner of the barn and disappeared. Del walked quickly after her to the driveway on the far side of the house. A woman leaned on a new car. She was petite, round figured, and wore high-heeled boots and makeup. She looked to be about his age, in her early thirties.

Anna greeted her. "Hi, Karen."

Karen had spied Del. "Is that Del Van-Orthrum? I heard you were back."

Del still couldn't place the woman, but at least he knew what to call her. "Hi, Karen."

Karen approached him with her arms flung wide. "Give me a hug. It's been years." After a quick clinch, she turned to Anna. "Del and I dated for a while back in high school."

Ah, now he placed her. They never actually dated, but they were only a year or two apart in school. "You were pals with my sister," he said.

"Maureen, yes. I haven't seen her in years. What's she up to?"

"She's a lawyer down in Bridgetown."

"Oh yeah," Karen drawled and gave Anna a quick look. "She practices family law. I used a guy in Kentville for my divorce."

Anna had her lips pressed together and her arms tightly crossed under her chest. Del had the impression that he was missing some kind of subtext, but he'd been gone from the Valley too long to be able to read it.

Karen asked, "When did you get back?"

"Last night."

"You want one flat or two today, Karen?" Anna asked, still looking impatient.

"Just one, thanks."

The moment Anna disappeared down a cellar door, Karen took Del's elbow, ostensibly to turn his back toward the house, and whispered, "Only back one day and already you're sniffing around Anna MacFrail?"

He stiffened. "I'm here on business."

"She finally selling out?"

"I don't know anything about that."

"Well, she should sell out before she does too much damage," she said, raising an eyebrow as if Del would understand her meaning.

He couldn't help himself—he wanted to know all about Anna. "She's not from around here, is she?"

"Lord, no. She's a city girl through-and-through. Decided to go back to nature and all that. Don't know why; she hasn't got a relaxed bone in her body. So you haven't heard about her, huh?"

"Dad said she'd been through some hard times."

She dropped her chin. "You talked to your father about her?"

He couldn't understand the innuendo. "I told you, we've got this . . . business thing."

"He didn't say anything else? About the two of them being . . . friendly?"

"What are you getting at, Karen?"

"Come on over to my house tonight and I'll explain the whole situation. It's best you hear it now, before you . . . make a big mistake."

"I think I know what you're implying, and you're way off base. My father's old enough to be her, well, father."

"And he's been a widower a good long time. Though why he'd choose a cold fish like her . . ."

"Here you go, Karen," Anna said, emerging from the house carrying a large flat of eggs protected by gray trays tied together with butcher's string.

"Put them on the backseat, will you dear?"

Anna nodded, expressionless. Del's heart pounded. Had she overheard what they were saying? He looked up at the trees, down at his sneakers, anywhere but at Anna.

Once the eggs were safely stored, Anna reached into her shirt pocket for an invoice book. "You want to pay for them now?"

"No, just put it on my bill."

Karen jumped into her car and started to back

up. She called out the window, "Seven o'clock, Del. Don't be late."

"Tonight? No . . . Karen, wait . . ."

Anna said something under her breath that sounded like "Don't be late."

Del asked, "Pardon?"

"Nothing."

"No, what did you say?"

"I shouldn't have let her leave without settling her account."

He watched Anna stride back toward the barn. Was it true? Were Anna and his father dating? That would explain her comment that morning about how if anyone would know the value of her land, he would. But she hadn't said anything about it. And, she didn't know that Nanny was ill. If she'd been dating Orsen, he would have told her that, wouldn't he? And surely his sister, Maureen, would have mentioned it in one of their frequent talks.

Del breathed out so forcibly through his nose that he made a harrumph sound. Orsen Van-Orthrum was a church-going man, a pillar of the community. He wouldn't take up with a girl half his age. No way. The idea that people like Karen were gossiping about his father made Del squirm inside. A man's reputation meant something here in the Valley. It affected all aspects of his life, including his business.

Del realized he'd been staring at Anna, taking in every detail of the smooth way she moved and the shape of her calves under her jeans. Her shoulders were thin but broad and they looked hiked, as if she were tense. When she stepped out of sight behind the barn, he felt let down.

Chapter Three

Anna, still damp and warm from her bath and cozy in a terry robe, curled up in the big arm-chair and reached over to snap on the reading lamp. She'd done a lot of thinking since that morning about how to handle the contaminated field. There was no point in being angry about it. The damage was done, and she'd just have to wait another three years before getting the field certified again. The question now was how much to charge Suffenbrook Farms. She could estimate what she'd get at the market if she sold the crop as organic, then subtract the return from selling the remaining plants as non-organic, and charge Del the difference. The problem was, she didn't have any contact with regular wholesalers. Would she be able to arrange a market between now and harvest? Her crop was so small compared to the big guys like Suffenbrook Farms, that no one was interested in her.

She dropped her head back and closed her eyes. Maybe this was a blessing in disguise? If Del gave her cash now, she could bring her checking account balance back up to zero. The more she thought about that, the better it sounded. She'd be able to buy the poultry feed in bulk; that would save a lot of money.

Del VanOrthrum. There was something so appealing about the man that he frightened her. It was an instinctive reaction, like a deer shying away from eating poison berries. Anna did not like to be frightened. It made her surly and quiet and, she had to admit to herself, unattractive.

The phone rang. Who could be calling at ten at night? She padded over to pick up the receiver.

"Anna, this is Karen Smyth. Is Del there?"

"Del VanOrthrum?"

"Well, of course, Del VanOrthrum. Do you know any other Dels? Well? Is he?"

"No, Karen. He's not."

"Do you know where he is?"

"No, why should I?"

"When did he leave your place?"

"Right after you did. Is there something wrong, Karen?"

"I don't take kindly to being stood up."

Anna felt a bubble of compassion. "This is a busy time of year. Maybe—"

"Don't you go making excuses for him. The man was a louse back in high school. I don't know why I thought he had changed." Click.

Anna found herself half-smiling. She liked that Del hadn't gone over to Karen's for dinner. In fact, the notion of the two of them all cozy had chafed in the back of her mind all afternoon. Oh no. She abruptly caught her thumbnail between her teeth. She was jealous. About Del VanOrthrum. Oh, this was terrible.

Del's father, Orsen, knew some of what Anna had been through, some of the terrible things she'd been accused of doing, but he didn't know the whole story. Maureen, Del's sister, probably knew everything but she was, apparently, too much of a professional to go blabbing about her clients. Judging by the look that Karen had given Anna that afternoon, she did know everything. And Karen had set her sights on Del VanOrthrum. No, it would be out-and-out stupid for Anna to have romantic thoughts about the man.

Anna paced back and forth on her worn Persian carpet droning an old show tune about washing a man right out of her hair.

Right about this time, Del and Mike Connor were packing up the tools after repairing the bearings on one of the John Deere tractors. Mike had been with the VanOrthrum farm since Del was a kid, working his way up from seasonal laborer to foreman. He didn't have much education beyond junior high school, and hadn't traveled further than the city of Halifax, an hour or so away, but he knew his job through and through. Del's father had often said how much he depended on Mike.

"Ya see," Mike said, "you can use either a flange or cast housing. Those three lips keep out the dirt but let the oil grease get purged from the heart of the bearing and the new stuff can still get in."

Del felt his eyes glaze over. He didn't know anything about this sort of thing. "As long as it works."

"Don't be discouraged. You'll pick it up," Mike said, tossing a rag to him.

"I think we're going to have to leave the farm machinery in your capable hands." He rubbed at his skin, but the dirt and grease had worked under his fingernails.

Mike watched him silently for a couple of

minutes, then asked, "Are you going to stay on for long once your dad gets back?"

"Depends on how long he's gone. I'll probably stay through the summer either way. I told a friend he could use my apartment until September."

Del waited at the door while Mike switched off the lights. He'd forgotten how many stars a person could see out here in the country. The very sight took some of the tension out of his shoulders.

"Heard you had some trouble over at Havenville."

Del groaned. "I was wondering when you'd bring that up."

"I was here last night too. I meant to say something, but we went onto the next thing and it slipped my mind."

Del smiled, thinking that was a kind thing for Mike to say. Nevertheless, he made the mistake, so he shouldered the responsibility. "Any suggestions about how to set things right?"

"Well now," Mike drawled, rubbing the back of his neck with a beefy hand, "most people would wait till harvest time, see what a load of cabbage is going for."

There was a light over the parking area between the house and the barn, but Mike stood with his back to it so Del couldn't see his expression.

"You think that's what I should do?" Del said.

"A fella could do that."

Now Del remembered one of the things that always bothered him about the farmers in the Valley. They didn't want to give advice straight out, so they danced around the topic as if it were disrespectful to voice an opinion.

"I'd like to get this settled before then," Del offered.

"I can see how you'd want that."

"Do you think the MacFrail woman will make trouble over this?"

"Not on purpose, no. I can't see her going to the police or nothing. But a person on the edge, well . . ."

The police? That hadn't even occurred to Del. "Do you know her, Mike?"

"Me? No, not me."

"Does my father?"

"You could say that."

"Are they friends?" Del couldn't seem to come right out and ask if his father and Anna were personally involved.

"I've seen her up here a time or two."

Mike didn't move toward his truck, just kept

staring off into the darkness, so Del asked, "What's her story?"

"You remember Chris Parker?"

"Doesn't ring a bell."

"Donald and Marge Parker's boy." Mike hawked and spit. "The summer he came home from Agricultural College, he brought that girl with him. Engaged, they were, but guess it didn't work out. Chris moved out west some-wheres. She stayed on."

"And she and my dad became friends?"

Mike abruptly started toward his truck. "I wouldn't say friends. Orsen felt sorry for her. Tried to help her out some. She made a big mistake buying that place down in Havenville. Run-down. I hear she paid twice what it was worth."

"When was this?"

"Five, six years ago."

"That long? She can't be more than twenty-three, twenty-four, now."

Mike jumped into his truck and said through the open window, "Don't know what her parents were thinking letting a little girl like that make such a big mistake."

After Mike left, Del felt like sitting down right there in the dirt, he was so physically tired, but his brain clicked over what Mike had said. Of course his father and Anna weren't dating. Anna likely needed an older, more experienced farmer to turn to now and again. That's all. Now he couldn't even understand why he gave the idea any credence in the first place. The girl seemed to get him all churned up inside so he couldn't think straight.

Mike had implied that Anna had financial problems. It didn't surprise him. Even big farms with a fortune in backing and the advantage of economy-of-scale were having a hard time of it these days.

His stomach growled from hunger, so he dragged himself into the house. When he opened the refrigerator door, he left a smudge of grease on the handle. It sparked a sudden memory of his mother scolding his father for that very thing. She'd been gone for over a decade now, a victim of breast cancer, but he still missed her. He thought how hard it must be for his father to go about his life alone in this big house. But, his days were busy, at least in the summer, and he went to Florida and golfed all winter.

Thinking about his father reminded him of his ailing grandmother. He grabbed a block of cheese and a bottle of beer, then plopped on the chair at the desk. His fingers were so stiff from holding tools all evening that it took three tries to twist off the bottle cap. He lifted the telephone receiver to check if his dad had left a message and heard the tell-tale beep, beep, beep.

Alarmed, he punched in the voicemail number and heard that he had three new messages. They were all from Karen Smyth, each one more angry-sounding than the last, all of them demanding that he call as soon as he got in. Relieved that there wasn't any bad news about his grandmother, he jotted down Karen's number and called.

"Well, it's about time," she said stiffly. "I was getting worried."

"Karen, I never said I'd be by this evening. You rushed off without giving me a chance."

"You could have called."

"I tried, but your number isn't in the book and there wasn't a listing on 411."

"I'm still going by my married name." She sounded calmer. "Why didn't you call my parents?"

Del had thought of that, but he didn't want to talk to them and start a rumor that he was dating Karen. Folks who were native to the Valley tended to expect their offspring to marry one another. "I'm sorry about the misunderstanding, but I'm so tied up here at the farm, I can't think about socializing right now. I hope you didn't go to too much trouble."

"Well, I suppose I can forgive you this time. But you'll have to make it up to me."

"Yeah, okay. See you."

"Goodnight, Del," she said, her voice honey-sweet. "Call me."

Would he call her? Maybe. He looked around the kitchen, at the dishes piled on the counter and the floor scuffed with the dirt he'd just tracked in. The fridge suddenly stopped its loud humming. The grandfather clock in the hallway ticked . . . ticked . . . ticked. Yeah, a guy could get lonely out here in the country.

Del spent the next few days getting all the parts that make a farm run smoothly and assembling them into some kind of order. He inspected the fields, checked over machinery, bought chemicals and fertilizers, and, during the long evenings, bent over the computer working out the payroll and paying bills. It was time to reward himself, so early one morning he announced that he'd cultivate the Havenville fields himself that day.

He climbed up into the cab of the tractor and whistled in pleasant surprise. Things had changed since he was a kid. The seat was as plush as any armchair.

Mike leaned past him, pointing out the features. "That there's the phone. You've got your temperature control here."

Del snapped open a cabinet. "Next you're going to tell me that this is refrigerated to keep my lunch cool."

Mike chuckled. "Haven't been able to talk Orsen into that feature yet."

Del flicked up a lever. "The air conditioning is a good idea. I remember when I was a kid, it felt like I was cooking out there in the fields."

After a few more pointers from Mike, Del drove the tractor out onto the paved road. He felt like a child behind the wheel of a giant toy. The steering was fast and responsive and he quickly brought the speed almost to the limit. Riding up there, with the twenty-square-foot windshield wrapped around him, he had a totally different perspective on the countryside. The dawn mist had cleared off, leaving a pale blue sky with wisps of clouds in the shape of galloping horses' tails. He looked down on an apple orchard. The blossoms were gone now, but the leaves were so fresh and green he had to smile with the pleasure of just looking at them.

Del hadn't realized, all those years locked away with his studies and business, that he missed the country. He told himself not to get too used to it; he'd be back in Toronto in a couple of months.

Ten minutes later he turned up the dirt road that formed the border between his carrot field and Anna's property. His mood dropped a notch when he saw the swatch of windswept red dirt where her crops had been. That debt hadn't been settled yet because she hadn't called, but he still had the folded blank check in his wallet.

He climbed down from the cab and walked the carrot field, comparing the plants in the treated section with those that the sprayer hadn't yet reached. There was no doubt in his mind that the plants competing with the robust weeds were having a hard go of it. They were smaller and a paler green. Even after he cultivated between the rows he'd have to send in people to do the close weeding. It seemed a pointless way to do business considering that all those man-hours would eat up any profit this crop produced.

Del admired anyone who followed their convictions, assuming that their actions didn't hurt anyone else. However, he couldn't help a niggling worry about the public mood against modern farming methods. Farmers were having a hard enough go of it without feeling the pressure to give up the few tools they had at their disposal, like herbicides, fungicides, insecticides. There was a lot of them-against-us attitude in the farming community. He hoped that Anna MacFrail had some other organic farmers to keep her company, because there was a pretty good chance that she was a *them* and not an *us* around the valley.

An hour later he took one hand off the wheel and slipped a different CD into the player. Another country-western singer's voice filled the cab. He'd have to remember to bring some of his own music next time. But he had to admit, now that he'd heard the tunes a few times, they were beginning to grow on him. In fact, they sounded a lot like old rock-and-roll music, which he really liked.

He'd just rounded the northern end of the field and was making the turn to line up with a new section when he saw Anna MacFrail running full-out down the slope from the man-made irrigation pond. She was too far off for him to see her face, but he knew something was wrong. She looked as if the devil was nipping at her heels. He performed a tight turn, running the tractor right over the corner of the carrot field, and shifted into high gear to rush toward her.

"What's wrong?" he called, stopping a few yards from her and shoving open the door.

"My cat," she said, gasping. "Something savaged it. I've got to get my truck."

"Get in."

She ran around the front of the tractor and climbed up to the cab. He got a good look at her face then, white and anxious. The sight of her eyes brimming with tears tore at his gut. Before she'd hauled the door shut, he started off again and headed right over the grain field toward the irrigation pond. The ruts from the wheels would be left there for everyone to see. He'd feel like a fool later, he knew, but at that moment he didn't care. He just wanted to some-how stop her tears.

Chapter Four

"Hold on," Del said as the tractor bumped over the field.

"She's just up there." Anna pointed toward the pond. "I . . . I didn't want to carry her all the way."

"Look in that cabinet. Maybe there's a rag or something we can put it in."

"Her," she said softly. Ricky was a she, a female.

She grabbed a grease-stained towel as Del slowed the tractor at the foot of the rise. The four-foot jump to the ground jarred her knees, but she hoofed it up the hill without slowing. Ricky lay on her side in a thicket of brambles and wild roses. Her little pink tongue moved up and down as she panted.

"How did you ever find it?" Del asked, stamping the brambles down to make room.

"I heard her howling." She'd been back at the pond priming the pump so she could water the new transplants as soon as she had them in the ground.

It took every bit of Anna's will power not to cry herself when Ricky yowled in pain as they picked her up and gently set her on the make-shift stretcher. The fur on her back leg was matted and sticky with dark blood, and the leg hung at an impossible angle.

Back in the cab of the tractor, Del handed Anna the cell phone so she could call the vet. They transferred to Anna's truck for the drive in. She sat in the passenger seat with Ricky on her lap while Del drove. The fact that her cat's ears were hot seemed like a very bad sign to her, but she gritted her teeth and remained silent. She would not cry in front of Del VanOrthrum. People in this valley scorned women who cried; she knew that from hard experience.

The vet took them right into an examining room and gave Ricky a shot for the pain. Then he carried her away, through the inner door, to the operating room.

Del pressed his hand on Anna's shoulder. "We might as well wait out here, huh?"

Feeling dazed, she allowed him to guide her to a chair in a waiting room that smelled of antiseptic and dried dog food. A woman sitting kitty-corner to her smiled sadly. She must have seen them carrying Ricky in. Anna was so afraid she had to sit on her hands to keep them from shaking.

"You okay?"

She couldn't bring herself to look at Del's face. If he showed any compassion, she'd crack. "Yeah. Listen, you take the car back to the farm. I'll hang around here and call a friend or someone when . . . when I'm done here." What friend? She didn't know anyone well enough to call in the middle of a workday. Her only close friend, Diana, would be manning the cash register at the store for the rest of the day. Maybe there was a taxi.

"Why don't I wait and see what the doctor says? Then we can drive back together."

His voice implied that it wouldn't be long. Did he think Ricky was going to die? Was there a washroom she could escape to? She just wanted him to go, but she was afraid to form the words in case she lost what little composure she had.

He shifted in his seat. "I'm pretty sure they'll want to keep it for observation."

A few minutes later the vet appeared and motioned for them. "It's not good. Her leg is badly crushed."

"You can't set it?" Del asked.

"I'm not confident that I can. We'll have to wait for the X rays, and even then . . ."

"And if the leg is too far gone? What then?"

"Then the only way to save the cat would be to amputate."

Del asked, "Can a cat live with only three legs?"

"Sure. They adapt very well."

Anna listened, horrified. Could she put Ricky through that much suffering? Shouldn't she tell this doctor to let her kitty stay asleep forever? Then she thought about the little pink nose and the way she snuggled in beside her on chilly nights. She was more than a cat, more than a friend; she was really like Anna's only family.

Del turned to her. "What do you want to do?"

Before she could answer, the doctor said, "Either way, I want to operate now."

Then the doctor told them how much it would cost and Anna felt the tears streaming down her face. She didn't have that kind of money, even if she maxed out her credit cards. Del put his arm around her shoulder and pulled her to him.

She breathed in jerky gasps, trying not to make a sound.

"Please," Del said to the doctor, "perform the operation."

"B . . . but I c . . . can't afford it."

"Don't worry about that now," he said. Then he nodded at the doctor. "We'll call you later."

Anna pushed herself from him. "Wait. Wait." She spied a box of tissue on the counter, grabbed a handful, and blew her nose. When she had herself under control, she said, "I don't want Ricky to suffer. Are you sure this operation will work? Will she be able to live pain-free afterward even if she . . . even if she loses the leg?"

"There could be complications, but her pelvic area looks unharmed."

Anna felt nauseous. How could she let Ricky die just because of money? Maybe she could sell the tractor, or her truck. She nodded. "Okay."

During the ride back to the farm, Anna felt dazed, and a sinus headache throbbed between her eyes. She risked a glance at Del. His thick brows were low over his eyes, and his lips formed a grim line.

"Sorry about all the trouble," she said.

"I'd love to get my hands on the animal that did that. I'd wring its neck."

Wasn't that just what a man would say. "Thank you for doing this."

He looked her fully in the eye. "You're welcome."

When he pulled into place in front of Anna's barn, Del said, "Arc you okay? Is there anything I can do for you? Make you a cup of coffee?"

"No, thank you. I think we should get back to work." She had to keep productive now more than ever.

He kept the key in his hand. "Listen, I know that the vet bill's going to be really big, so do you think we should settle the over-spraying thing now?"

She didn't want him to know about her dire financial situation. It was bad enough that he'd seen her cry. "I haven't had a chance to think about that yet."

"How about a partial payment?"

"All right." She motioned toward his hand. "Just put the key under the mat."

"Under the mat?"

"By your feet."

"Aren't you afraid someone will steal your truck?" He stopped and looked at the torn roof fabric and dented dashboard. Then he slipped the key under the mat with a look that said *who would want to steal this?*

This truck might be shabby looking, Anna fumed, but it was the only one she had. It was easy for him to sneer; he obviously had lots of money. "What do you do for a living?"

"I teach business subjects at a community college in Toronto. Why do you ask?"

Now she regretted the personal question, so she blurted the first thing that came into her head: "Your hands are soft," and left the car.

Cringing on the inside, Anna marched around the barn down to where she'd left the flatbed parked. Del had just seen her through a terrible ordeal, and what did she do? She insulted him.

The sun had moved around, so the fragile transplants now seared under it. She quickly shoved off the flatbed's brake and pushed the whole thing further under the tree. Then she hauled the hose from the basement of the barn, attached the sprinkler, and gave the trays a good soaking. She felt too humiliated to look up when Del drove his tractor past her and up the dirt road.

Del felt confused. One minute Anna was a vulnerable, kind woman, the next minute she acted cold and insensitive. Was she ashamed that he'd seen her cry? Heck, after seeing what that poor cat had gone through, he'd almost blubbered himself. She was right about one thing, he did have soft hands. They were big enough, and the fingers were straight and long, but except for a couple of scraped knuckles, they looked like hands that had never seen a day's work.

He sat in his comfortable, air-conditioned tractor cab and drove sedately up and down the rows of carrots feeling peeved, until he noticed that Anna had her own tractor out—a vintage one by the look of its rounded mudguards and high seat. She was perched with her left hand on the wheel and her body twisted so she could look back and forth between the row ahead of her and the shallow furrow she was cutting behind her. He liked watching Anna, the way she sat so tall and confident in the seat with her long legs braced on the housing. A few minutes later his own work took him to the west side of the field where he couldn't see her, and the job suddenly seemed deadly boring.

When he finally finished, he drove back over to Anna. He intended to say a few words about the cat, perhaps ask if she'd had a chance to call the hospital to see how she came through the surgery.

He found Anna putting transplants in by hand. A flatbed carrying more plants had been pulled up and left on the dirt road nearby. With a tray of seedlings under one arm, she was hunched over, picking out one tiny plant at a time. Then she would drop it in the furrow and heel the soil around it with her work boots.

There was dirt smudged on her cheek, and long strands of hair had escaped her ponytail. She looked hot and discouraged.

At this rate she'd be done in about a week's time. He jumped down from the cab and strode over to the flatbed.

"Need a hand?" he asked.

"No, thank you." She didn't look up from her work.

"Next time you do some planting, you should rent the gear."

"Didn't figure there were enough to justify the expense. Besides, these plugs are too big for those shoots."

The plants did look leggy, and too big for the shallow amount of soil they were planted in. They were likely just left over from a greenhouse somewhere. He looked at the flatbed, then up at the clear, blue sky. "They're drying out."

"I know they're drying out," she snapped.

He felt like cringing under the force of her glare, but he smiled stiffly and joked, "Wouldn't you know we never have a cloud when we need it."

She made a noncommittal sound and dropped the last of the transplants from her tray into the ground. She heeled them in and marched back to get another tray.

"Listen, Anna. The least I can do is help you

plant these. After all, you wouldn't be doing it if I hadn't told Stubby to spray here."

"Stubby?" she said, incredulous.

"That's what he goes by."

She eyed the hundreds of seedlings yet to be planted, looked up at the sky, over to the field, then back at the plants.

"Come on, let me help you," he said again. "It would make me feel better."

"Won't change how much money I'm going to charge you."

The peak of her baseball cap shaded her eyes, but he had the impression that she was challenging him. He was tempted to say something snide about the weight of the chip she carried on her shoulders, but decided silence would be more prudent. He just nodded.

"Help me unload the trays alongside where I'll need them, then you can take the tractor and fetch the irrigation pipes." She motioned toward the pyramid of long aluminum conduits stacked by the copse of trees at the foot of the field. "It's a lot easier for two people to haul them into place than it is for one."

"No kidding," Del said. Each of those pipes had to weigh at least fifteen pounds.

"Do you suppose," Anna said, pulling another full tray so it balanced on her hip, "before you start, you could use that cell phone and call about Ricky?"

Chapter Five

Before Del called the veterinary hospital, he returned a message Mike had left.

"Where are you?" Mike asked.

"Over at Havenville."

"It took you five hours to cultivate that little field?"

"No, Anna's cat got hurt and I helped her take it to the vet."

Mike took a moment to answer. "We've been waiting on the tractor down here."

"Right. Sorry. Can you send someone down to get it?"

"Why can't you drive it back yourself?"

Del rubbed the back of his neck. "I could, but . . . is there anyone else there at the farm?"

"I put Stubby in the shed stenciling the bulk bins."

"Get him to drive up the car and take the tractor. I'll bring the car home with me when I'm done here."

"Done doing what, Del?"

"I offered to lend Anna a hand."

"You offered to lend her a hand. Without checking with me? Do you have any idea of what an hour of that tractor's time is worth?"

Del had swiveled around so he could watch Anna. She'd never be able to rent a rig like the one he sat in, one that could take a swath four times the width of hers. Maybe he should offer to cultivate her fields for her? "I changed my mind," he said. "I'll bring the tractor back myself in a few hours."

"You bring it back right now," Mike barked. "You may be the owner's son, but I'm still the foreman around this place. What I say goes. I want to see that tractor pulling into the yard in ten-minutes time. Got that?"

It had been years since anyone spoke to Del with that tone. His initial impulse was to chuckle, then he realized he deserved Mike's scolding. He had been irresponsible. "You're right. I'm sorry. See you in ten minutes."

Del deeply regretted inconveniencing Stubby and Mike. It would have only taken a moment to let them know what was going on. Instead he forgot all about the farm, and about his promise to his father that he would look after things. This wasn't at all like him; he had always thought of himself as pretty considerate of other people.

He shook aside his own embarrassment and phoned the vet. The news there was heartening. Ricky had fared better during the operation than they had expected. He hurried over to tell Anna.

"They were able to save her leg," he said. Anna emitted a huge sigh of relief. Del continued, "They want to keep her overnight, but we . . . you can pick her up in the morning."

"She must have a cast on."

"Expect so."

She shifted the weight of the seedling tray on her hip as if she wanted to get back to work. "I . . . ah . . . thanks."

"No problem. Listen, I have to return the tractor."

Disappointment flickered in her eyes, then her face took on the carefully blank expression that Del now recognized as a mask.

"I understand. Thanks again for helping me with the cat." She bent to set another plant in the furrow.

"I'll come back as soon as I can."

"See you."

She didn't think he would return, Del realized, annoyed. There she was, with hundreds of seedlings about ready to die from the heat, and she couldn't even ask for help.

As he drove back to the farm he wondered what life had been like for Anna MacFrail. What made her so determined to do everything herself? Then he realized that Anna shouldn't have had to ask for help. Her neighbors had eyes. Didn't they see what she was going through? All his life Del believed that the people in the country were more neighborly than those in the city. If a family got themselves into a fix, their friends pitched in and helped them over the rough spot. What happened to the good people of the Valley? What happened to old-fashioned charity?

The other side of that country coin was that people native to the Valley tended to mistrust those 'from away.' If your parents and grandparents hadn't been born here, you couldn't expect to be totally accepted. Two people meeting for the first time almost always set about to establish one another's family trees. Where are you from? Who are your parents? Didn't my cousin marry your sister's husband's . . . ? Folks in the Valley didn't air their family secrets with anyone from away either. They solved their problems among themselves, and only called in the authorities—like the police or government officials—if other people in the family couldn't set things right.

Poor Anna was excluded from the inner circle.

Mike, who must have heard the tractor coming up the drive, met him in the yard. He looked irritable.

"Mike," Del said, heading him off. "I'm sorry about the tractor. Don't know what got into me."

"I do."

"Huh?"

"You got distracted by a pretty face."

Del pulled himself up taller. "I don't appreciate the implication. I hardly know the woman."

"I didn't mean any disrespect to Anna."

"What would you have done?" he demanded. "Let the cat die? With her looking on, crying?"

Mike's eyebrows shot up. "Anna MacFrail cried?"

"You people seem to think she's made of steel. Is that why you've let her die a slow death down there in Havenville?" Mike looked startled. "Do you know what she's doing right now? She's putting in hundreds of plants *by hand*. She's replacing the plants *we killed*."

"Why didn't you say so?"

"So I'm going back to help her. If some of my own work gets neglected, so be it."

"I'll get Stubby."

"I'll even hire extra help out of my own pocket if . . ." He stopped when Mike's words penetrated his brain.

Mike spoke over his shoulder, "With the three of us lending a hand, we should be through in no time."

Anna considered herself to be in good physical condition; the muscles in her arms felt like coils of thick hemp rope from the constant lifting and dragging she did. Nevertheless, this day's labor could very well defeat her. Her lower back burned from the repetitive bending and straightening, but she'd tried crawling along on her knees until they ached with bruises. The muscles in her neck had kinks from carrying the heavy trays of plants.

Perhaps she should drive the flatbed back under the tree down by the barn and give the plants another drink? She squinted up at the sun; only a couple of more hours of daylight left. When she bent again, her head swam. Low blood sugar. She hadn't eaten anything since before dawn.

A vehicle pulled up behind her and Anna's heart lurched. Del did come back. Still, rather than turning, she continued her relentless planting. She wasn't at all sure she'd be able to maintain her composure if she looked at him. Another bout of tears threatened. Not only that, with her hair all askew and her face bright red, she probably looked like a bad case of heat rash.

Then she heard men's voices. Her curiosity got the better of her and she staggered around. He'd brought two men with him.

"Anna," Del said. "Hope you don't mind, but Mike and Stubby wanted to come and help too."

The older man strode forward with his hand outstretched. "Mike Connor. I'm the foreman at the VanOrthrum place. I believe we met a time or two."

Anna shifted the tray to her other arm so she could return the handshake. She did recognize this gray-haired man from one of the Vegetable Grower Association meetings. He'd never given her the time of day before; just been one of the dozens of farmers who she ran into at those things. But Del had said they came to help?

"You've already met Stubby," Mike added, indicating the round-bellied man who stood next to a two-ton long-bodied truck. "I figure he can pull the irrigation pipes into place. If that's okay with you?"

Her tongue felt too thick for her mouth. "I'd be . . . that would be . . . Thank you."

She felt grateful when Mike simply nodded and turned away to give Stubby directions. They were being so kind, and she wasn't used to kindness. In fact, over the previous few years she'd learned to shun it because it generally imposed an obligation worth far more than the original act. She told herself she didn't owe them a thing. After all, she wouldn't be in this jam if they hadn't over-sprayed her field. When it came time for them to leave, she'd politely thank them for the help, but she wouldn't gush. Never.

Two hours later, Anna gazed at her field, dazed. The plants were all tucked in the soil, and revolving sprinklers showered droplets over their young leaves. She stepped over to the first row for a closer look, dropped to her haunches, and braced her fingers on the damp, sandy loam. The tiny heart-shaped seed leaves already stiffened with water.

When the sprinklers approached again, Anna started to get up, but her thighs quivered with exhaustion. Suddenly a firm hand grasped her elbow and lifted her to a standing position. She and Del backed out of the way of the water.

"I never could tell the difference between cole crops. What are these?"

"Cabbage. They have rounder leaves than broccoli and cauliflower. Darker green."

"How do you plan to control pests without chemicals?"

"I spray BT to control the caterpillar."

"BT?"

"It's a naturally occurring bacterium. Turns the caterpillars into mush."

"Using a bacterium sounds just as potentially dangerous to the environment as spraying with a chemical that's been well-tested."

"Right now, I don't have the energy to explain it."

He smiled. "Maybe over dinner sometime?"

Anna blinked up at him. Had Del just asked her out? She could almost hear her friend Diana's voice telling her to go for it. Should she? Probably not. A guy that good-looking had to be trouble. She made a noncommittal sound and turned away.

The two-ton truck bumped down the road toward them with Mike and Stubby in the front seat. When it stopped, Anna leaned in the window.

"I was awfully happy to hear the water gurgling down those pipes," she said.

"I can see you've been trying to look after that there pump," Mike replied, "but she's pretty old."

Anna agreed. "The irrigation system came with the place." She felt lucky to have one at all, considering the cost of those outfits.

"Don't suppose we'll get rain tonight."

It was, Anna knew, his way of asking how long she'd leave the sprinklers on. "I'll come out later this evening and shut it down."

Mike nodded as if she'd given a correct answer.

Stubby shifted over to let Del join them in the front seat, then the two of them scrunched down to peer out the window at her. They looked far less threatening like that.

"Thank you very much, guys, for helping me out here."

"Least we can do." Mike shoved the car into drive. "Hop on the back and we'll give you a lift down to the road."

Anna stood on the rear bumper and held onto the truck's tailgate. North Mountain was silhouetted by a peach-colored sky so the softwood trees along its ridge looked like tiny black spearheads. She looked out over her own field. The plants she'd set weeks earlier had grown so that now distinct lines of green followed the contours of the red soil. From now on she'd have to spend at least a couple of hours in the cool mornings each day hoeing up those lines, keeping the weeds at bay until the plants were mature enough to overshadow any competition.

The truck stopped. Anna jumped down and waved a good-bye.

The chicken run was empty, as the hens all

roosted with the arrival of evening. She moved the bracing irons and shoved the big double doors closed. Other than the dull hum of the pump running in the irrigation pond way up past the far end of the fields, there wasn't a sound. As she walked through the gloom between the house and barn, she realized that she watched for Ricky's shadowy form to come bounding toward her as she did every night. Poor Ricky.

The house loomed black and silent and lonely. Despite all the lectures Anna inflicted upon herself, she still wanted someone in her life, someone who would make sure that the porch light was on when she came in from work. Perhaps she should go out with Del—if he ever asked her again—but the thought of opening herself up to that kind of risk made her cringe. Anna's heart had been through so much already. She wouldn't survive another betrayal. Besides, Del's sister represented Chris's family during that terrible scandal. She knew everything. If Anna dated Del, would his sister feel compelled to tell him all about her? To expose her?

No, it would be better for everyone if Anna MacFrail kept to herself.

Chapter Six

The Valley Vegetable Growers Association met the first Wednesday of every month in a hall at the Agricultural Research Station. Anna rarely attended, but she'd heard that the group had received a grant from the government to help offset the cost of bulk bins, the big wooden boxes that apple and vegetable growers filled when they harvested their produce. Anna figured her annual membership dues gave her the right to buy some of these inexpensive bins.

She fastened her hair at the back of her neck with a clip, and pulled on some clean jeans and the blouse she'd just ironed. The waistband of the pants drooped around her hips.

"I've got to start eating better," she said to

Ricky. The cat lounged on the bed with one leg stuck out in an ungainly cast.

She scooped the cat into her arms and carried her down the steep staircase to the kitchen. When she set her carefully on the floor, Ricky hopped awkwardly over to a sunny spot on the braided rug and sprawled out. Anna smiled at her. Other than the first day, when her eyes were glazed with fear and pain, Ricky had adapted very well to her condition. In fact, she seemed to like being carried in and out from the barn and having her food dish delivered to wherever she happened to flop. Anna ran her hand over the warm, soft fur and smiled when a deep purr erupted. After making sure Ricky's milk and food were within easy reach, she left for the meeting.

Only about fifty people milled around the large hall. Anna smiled at a circle of women she recognized as being some of her egg customers. Then she took a seat at the end of a row and stared forward, waiting for things to get underway.

A male voice spoke her name. Anna turned to see Del closing in on her. He looked bigger here than he did in the wide open fields, taller, broader in the shoulders. The sleeves of the golf shirt he wore stretched around his biceps. She experienced a fleeting moment of pleasure thinking that he sought her out, until she remembered Del probably didn't know any more people there than she.

"This seat taken?" he asked, pointing to the chair next to her.

Anna had to smile; there wasn't anyone else sitting within two rows of her. "Help yourself."

"How's the cat doing?"

"She's getting fat and spoiled."

"You get my check?"

"Yes, thanks." The money had allowed her to bail Ricky out of the veterinary hospital.

"You'll let me know if it's not enough?"

Del had been more than generous, so she doubted that the VanOrthrum farm owed her more, but it seemed prudent to wait and see.

"Hey, Del!" A man with a prematurely receding hairline waved from a seat at the front.

"Hi, Bob," Del called back. "How's it going?"

"How come nobody told me you was back?"

Heads turned. A couple of faces smiled back. Another man, this one far to the right, shouted, "Because we like him!" A few people guffawed.

"Bring your friend and come on and sit with us," Bob yelled.

Del grinned and started to stand. "Come on."

Anna demurred, unsure of her best course. "You go ahead. I don't know those people."

Del grabbed her hand. "Good a time as any to meet them."

He dragged her up to the front row. As soon as they stopped, she pried her hand free. Inside, Anna squirmed, but she kept a smile pasted on her face and concentrated on saying hello at appropriate times. It was homecoming week for Del.

"Is that you, Elizabeth?" he said to a tall woman with over-permed hair and a square chin.

"I'm married to Bob now, Del."

"Now that's taking Christian charity a bit far, Elizabeth!" More laughter.

"You home for good, Del?"

"Just the summer while Dad's over helping his mother out."

The smile had slipped from Anna's face. She realized that Elizabeth had noticed.

"You two known each other long?" When Anna shook her head, Elizabeth smiled knowingly. "Just a summer romance, eh?"

Anna shook her head. She was about to explain that their fields abutted one another when a voice growled from behind her back.

"Del VanOrthrum, I want a word with you."

Anna froze. She recognized that voice. An avalanche of terrible memories assailed her.

Del said, "I don't believe we've met?"

"Donald Parker. I know your father."

"What can I do for you, Mr. Parker?" Del asked coolly.

"Excuse me," Anna said quickly, but Elizabeth, who was watching Del and Donald Parker with wide eyes, didn't appear to hear her.

Anna left the hall using a side door, walked the long way around the building, and reentered at the back where no one could see her. She'd decided years earlier that the best way to handle Donald and Marge Parker was to avoid them. Luckily, she liked sitting alone at the back, where she could observe everyone else and be invisible herself.

Someone tapped on a microphone, and everyone settled in their seats. Anna couldn't see Del, but she assumed that he stayed in the front with his old friends.

If she ever went back to Ottawa, where she grew up, would she run into old high school friends? Likely, but she didn't intend to go back there. Anna's parents died while she attended Agricultural College and she, as an only child, had no brothers and sisters to visit. When she graduated, she followed her fiancé, Chris Parker, to the Valley, and rashly spent her inheritance on the farm in Havenville.

It was Chris' father, Donald Parker, who wanted to talk to Del. No doubt he would warn

Del about seeing her. Most people just rolled their eyes when the old guy ranted, as if they didn't believe his stories. Even so, it had been Anna's experience that they didn't remain friends with her for long. Perhaps she just wasn't worth the aggravation.

Back up at the front of the hall, Del stewed. He leaned over to Elizabeth and whispered, "Where did Anna go?"

Elizabeth hissed back, "Anywhere that Donald Parker wasn't, I imagine."

"Why?"

"The old guy hates her."

"Because she dumped his son?"

She eyed him as if she didn't believe he hadn't heard the story. "It's a little more complicated than that."

He leaned back in the hard metal chair and turned his attention to the podium. Oh no. Apparently Donald Parker was the president of the Vegetable Growers Association. He rapped a gavel on the wood and welcomed everyone to the meeting. Del knew, because his father had taken a turn or two as president, that the position rotated among the owners of the bigger farms in the Valley. Nevertheless, it did have some clout. Donald Parker couldn't be dismissed outright.

When the meeting broke up, Del wanted to

hurry out and find Anna. Instead he lingered at the front of the hall gossiping with his old school chums until Donald Parker motioned to him.

"How's your father?" Donald asked.

"Fine. I talked to him last night."

"That's good. Why don't we head toward the parking lot, eh?"

Once outside, Del scanned the lot for Anna's old truck, but couldn't see it under the glare of the overhead lights. Someone tooted a horn and he and Donald both lifted a hand to wave.

"I hear you're an accountant," Donald said.

"I teach business classes at a community college."

"My problem is, Del, that the treasurer this year don't know diddly about bookkeeping. I was wondering if you'd lend him a hand."

"I'm only here for a few more months, Donald."

"He just needs someone to get him straightened away."

"Sure then. I'll be happy to help. Why don't you arrange a meeting for us?" They stopped halfway down the parking lot. By now, most of the vehicles were gone.

"It would be better if you called him yourself and offered your services. More subtle, if you know what I mean." Donald pulled a slip of paper from his pocket. "Here's his name and phone number."

Del shoved it in his trousers. He wasn't surprised when Donald stayed where he was, staring into shadowy bushes. Clearly the man had something on his mind and Del had a pretty good idea what it was.

"I see you're friendly with that Anna Mac-Frail," Donald said finally.

"Our Havenville fields border hers."

"You know the girl's background?"

"I know some, Donald, but I like to make up my own mind about people."

"Your father is a friend of mine so I feel it's my duty to warn you about her."

Del realized he had crushed the slip of paper in his pocket. "Don't go to the trouble," he said, struggling to keep his tone noncommittal. "If you figure there's something I ought to know, I'll ask my father."

"He doesn't know all the facts."

"Donald, I'm sure you mean well, but I'm not comfortable with this conversation."

"Someone like that doesn't belong in the Vegetable Growers' Association. We're getting together a petition to kick her out."

"Come on, she's just a lone person working her butt off on that miserable farm."

"She's out to get the rest of us."

"I think this conversation is over."

"She's a liar, and a scheming—"

"That's enough!" Del wanted to shove his fist in Donald's face.

Donald barked a cold laugh. "I see she's already got her claws into you."

"Do yourself a favor." Del jabbed Donald's shoulder with the tip of his finger. "Stop spreading this slanderous garbage."

He strode off toward his truck, but Donald followed and grabbed his arm. "You think this is fun for me? I'm only telling you for your own good."

"Don't bother, okay? I hardly know her."

Del climbed into his truck and started the motor, but he didn't put it into drive. He felt disgusted with himself, as much as with Donald Parker, because he didn't defend Anna. How could he? What he'd told Donald was true; he hardly knew the woman.

Chapter Seven

Warm milk and chocolate. Comfort food. Anna stirred the pan with a wooden spoon a few times, then reached into the cupboard for the cocoa. A sad, helpless feeling settled in her chest. She thought she had hardened herself to the Parkers and their malicious gossip, but the ache resurfaced.

"Sticks and stones may break my bones, but names will never hurt me."

The first year after Chris Parker ran off, Anna constantly teetered on the brink of crying. Feeling cheapened and helpless and full of regret, she had put the farm on the market. The selling price needed to be so high, to cover her mortgage and the debts, that there were no takers.

Over time, Anna learned to concentrate on her own small world. She straightened her back and figuratively thumbed her nose at Valley society. Her revenge would be the fact that she made a success of her little farm all by herself. She didn't need anyone else's approval.

A little part of her still felt as if she deserved all the bad luck that came her way. Oh, she rationalized it, of course. It wasn't totally her fault. Nevertheless, the Parker family did suffer because of her well-intentioned but misguided interference. She wondered if Donald Parker was telling Del about that right now. If so, would Del be understanding—the way Anna's friend, Diane, had been—or would he condemn her for meddling in someone else's business. Anna had meddled in Parker business. She did cause that family terrible anguish.

If only she could turn back time.

Anna groaned aloud. If only she'd had time to get to know Del before Donald Parker had a chance to poison him with his lies.

The big vase of peonies looked off center on the hand-woven tablecloth. She leaned over to rearrange them, shifting the stems so the white blossoms were mixed around the darker pink and rose-colored ones. This time of year she kept her house filled with their sweet aroma.

I must enjoy the little things, she told herself.

I must not let the past intrude. Anna had a tune she sang to herself whenever she found herself obsessing about the Parkers: *Rumination will be the ruination of me.*

A movement caught the corner of her eye. Ricky struggled to her feet and stared intently at the door. Someone was out there. At ten at night? Two sharp raps. Anna released a breath. An intruder wouldn't bother to knock; the door wasn't locked.

She flicked aside the gingham curtains over the kitchen door and saw Del's solemn face.

His voice was muffled through the glass. "I know it's late, but can we talk?"

"Where did you leave your truck?" she asked, opening the door.

He looked confused. "Up by the road."

"You're not afraid that word will get out that you visited the infamous Anna MacFrail at night?" Anna sounded bitter, but she couldn't seem to stop herself.

He sighed. "Guess you know that I had a talk with Donald Parker."

"I figured." There was no point in being churlish. "Come in. I'm just making hot chocolate. Would you like a cup?"

"Thank you."

She motioned toward one of the press-back

chairs. "You don't need to tell me what he said. I've heard it all."

"It's true then?"

She glared at him. "You don't know me, Del, so I'll let that slide." His chuckle surprised her. "What?"

"That's what I was just saying to myself. I don't know you, so I really don't know if you're a good person or not. Just because you look like an angel doesn't mean you are one."

The heat of a blush rushed up from her throat so she turned to get more milk from the refrigerator. It took a moment to measure it into the saucepan. When she turned back, Del had Ricky on his lap. His long fingers gently glided over the cat's orange fur.

He said, "She's purring. Guess it doesn't itch. I broke my leg when I was a kid. The cast nearly drove me crazy."

The light from a swag lamp hanging low over the center of the pedestal table illuminated the lower half of Del's face more than his eyes. A dark shadow cupped his chin and cheeks, showing he needed a shave. It made him look more fierce than usual, or perhaps it was the grim line of his mouth and the way his brows shadowed his eyes.

Del was so good-looking it made her nervous. She fought it by sounding irritated. "What part?"

"Huh?"

She fiddled with the mugs, chocolate, and milk. "You asked if it was true. Which part? The part where I tricked their son into proposing and then broke his heart?"

He scowled. "Maybe I shouldn't have come over here."

"Why did you?"

"Because I didn't believe the things he said. My gut reaction was to call him a filthy liar, but I didn't know the facts so I couldn't say anything."

She turned around and leaned back against the kitchen counter. "So you went to all this trouble to come to hear my side?"

"I should have guessed that you wouldn't want to talk about it."

She took a deep breath. "I'm sorry. You're being fair and I appreciate that. Do you really want to know what happened?"

"I do."

"Okay." She stirred the milk. "I met Chris Parker during my first year at Agricultural College." What a wide-eyed child she had been.

"How old were you?"

"Eighteen," she said, and smiled ruefully. "Thought of myself as a mature adult. He declared his love. Old story. Then my parents died.

I'm an only child, so I really leaned on Chris through all that."

As Anna talked, Del continued to stroke Ricky, but his eyes followed her every move. She found it disconcerting.

"Chris graduated that spring and I didn't want to lose him so I . . . weaseled a marriage proposal out of him. Oh, he loved me at the time, and he did give me his grandmother's ring and all. He brought me back to meet his parents."

She set out some bran muffins, small plates, knives, butter, and napkins.

"Thank you," Del said as she put the snack before him. "Did they like you?"

"At first, they were extremely kind to me. Oh, I think they thought we were too young, but they made the best of it."

"You were only a teenager."

"I suppose they felt sorry for me as I'd just lost my own parents. I went back to Ottawa and sold everything to an estate auction house. Then I transferred my money into a bank here. Chris and I had talked about buying a farm of our own, and I had the ready cash, so we started looking."

She glanced toward the big, north-facing window. It was night now so the semi-sheer drapes had been drawn, but she remembered the first time she'd looked out over the fields of grain undulating toward North Mountain. The view took her breath away. It still had the power to move her.

"This place was so pretty, I fell in love with it. I'd never bought anything big before. Compared to the prices in Ottawa, it seemed really inexpensive. I knew enough to bargain a little, but . . . I was so stupid about it."

"Did the Parkers help?"

"No, not really. I don't blame them for that, it was about this time of year and they were tied up with their own farm." Del didn't look convinced. "I moved over right away and started working it."

"Was it in both yours and Chris's names?"

"No," she said. "That was just a lucky blunder. The lawyer advised me and I figured it didn't matter. In my mind it belonged to both Chris and me."

"What shape was the place in then?"

"It hadn't been lived in for years. I battled spiders and houseflies for months. By that fall, I had covered every surface—paint, flooring, tiles. Spending more of my inheritance, I'm afraid."

He buttered a muffin and didn't look at her face as he asked, "Did you and Chris live here together?"

"No. He was helping his father with the cows

most of the time. It was hard work, and he hated it. Then on the weekends, I expected him to come over here and help me with this place." The milk smelled warmly sweet as she poured it into the mugs.

"That's when things started to go wrong?"

"He didn't have the same vision of the future as I did," she said, handing him a mug. "Pretty soon he wanted me to sell it. I wanted to buy a tractor."

"And you won."

She ignored that. "When I realized how he felt, I called a real estate agent. . . . That's when I found out how much over market value I'd paid." She took a sip of chocolate. "I could have sold out then, and been left with something."

"Do you wish you had?"

"I used to. But . . . oh this place got in my blood. You've got to admit, when you get past all the repairs it needs, this is a pretty farm."

He nodded and looked her straight in the eye. "One of the prettiest I've ever seen."

His look shook her, so she had to turn away and collect her thoughts. "Anyway . . . Chris and I started fighting. I was such a blithering optimist, you understand. It must have been so hard on him, me totally unaware of what he was going through. This place made me feel independent and strong; it made Chris feel trapped."

"Not everyone is cut out to be a farmer."

"All this," she continued, waving a hand to indicate the property, "overwhelmed him. Nothing was turning out the way we planned. He was only twenty at the time. And I knew I'd rushed him into getting engaged. It was, at least partially, my fault."

"So you broke up."

"Chris took off. His parents said I only got engaged to him so I could get this farm. They think I broke his heart."

"Why didn't you sell out then?"

"By then I'd bought the used tractor, so the debts to the property were bigger than I could get from a sale."

Del stood up and carried his empty mug to the sink. "But you know what the Parkers are saying about you?"

She nodded, but couldn't look him in the eye. Apparently Del didn't know *everything* that the Parkers were saying about her.

"Sure you hurt their son, but you were hurt too. They don't have any right to act this way. Why don't you set them straight?"

"What good would it do? People will think what they want to think."

"You've been dealt a raw deal. It's not right."

The constricted feeling in her chest abruptly relaxed. Del VanOrthrum was angry *for* her, not *at* her. Maybe things would turn out all right after all.

"You have to stand up for yourself, Anna. Who knows how these false accusations are affecting you. Maybe you'd be selling twice the number of eggs, or hearing about deals on—I don't know—" He hesitated and looked around as he searched for the right word. "Tractor tires."

"I've thought about it a lot. Making a fuss will do more harm than good."

"To the Parkers, maybe. Not to you."

"I have no wish to hurt the Parkers." Anna couldn't bring herself to tell Del the other things that Marge and Donald Parker believed she'd done.

"You'd change your tune if you heard the way he talked about you tonight." She flinched. "I'm sorry, that must hurt."

"It does hurt me, but I've tried telling my side of the story. Who do you suppose people believed? Me, a stranger from away, or the Parkers?"

He dropped to his haunches next to her and took each of her hands in his own. Surprised, she almost jerked them away. His eyes were as brown as the chocolate she'd mixed in with the milk, and tan lines radiated from the corners. He smelled faintly of soap.

"You've had a rough time of it," he said softly. "I don't know why that bothers me so much, but it does. I want to do something about it."

"Del, I . . . I can't open that wound again. I just can't."

"Next time I see Donald Parker, I'm going to tell him exactly how I feel."

She pulled her hands free from his and stood. "I wish you wouldn't, Del. I really wish you'd just forget all about it."

She tried to turn away from him, but Del cupped her cheek in one of his hands. It took an effort for her not to lean into that warm, comforting hand. Would he be so understanding if he knew everything? If pressed, Donald would tell Del the entire sordid story.

"Please don't mention it to the Parkers. Please."

Chapter Eight

For the next few days, everything seemed easier. The weeds practically climbed out of the ground as soon as Anna swung the hoe; the chickens laid larger eggs; and although it rained each night, the skies cleared by morning.

The hot sun baked her back as she shuffled along hilling up the potato plants, but Anna hummed happily. Her sandy soil was ideal for potatoes, so each spring she put in long rows of two varieties, one early and the other midseason. The new growth looked healthy, not a Colorado beetle in sight yet, but she knew they would soon appear. Then she'd have to schedule another hour a day to search through the plants to remove the bugs by hand.

"Anna?"

She straightened and smiled. "Over here."

Del appeared from between two grape rows. "I came to kidnap you to take you to lunch."

She looked down at her dusty clothes and shoes. The work made her so grimy that each night she ran water right from the outside hose over her feet because they were caked with dirt that seeped through her porous sneakers. "I don't know, Del. It would take me so long to get ready." He looked disappointed. "Unless we just went to a drive-through?"

"How about a fast-food joint?"

She leaned the hoe across her shoulder like a rifleman and strode toward him. "I'll just pop in the house and wash up." He was looking at the potatoes. "What?"

"I was thinking that I should bring down the John Deere and hill those up for you. It would be so much faster."

Her first impulse was to snap that she didn't need anyone's free handouts, then she reconsidered. Del was just being neighborly. Nevertheless, she wouldn't take him up on his offer. "Thanks anyway, but I'm selling these as organic. It's against the rules to use a tractor that might have chemicals or whatever on it."

"I could hose it down first."

"If I wanted to use a tractor, I'd use my own.

I do have a horse-hoe." She regretted her sharp tone. "Besides, it'll only take me another half hour to finish up."

"A horse hoe. That's the thing with the disks, isn't it?"

She smiled. "You fancy farmers haven't used them for years, but they do the trick for me."

"You work so hard, Anna. I wish I could help."

"Just having you as my friend is a big help." Suddenly shy, she looked down at the ground. She'd only spoken the truth, but the unguarded way she'd blurted it out shocked her. Something about Del made her forget to keep her guard up.

They passed through the rows of grape trellises. "What's the story with these?"

"It's a test plot. This is such good south-facing bottom land that I think it will grow grapes well."

"Where will you sell them? To the vineyard?"

"Most people are selling them there, but I didn't plant a wine grape. These are going to be sweet, for table or juice."

"And organic?"

"Of course." He frowned. "You don't approve?"

"I'm not against it, it just seems the hard way to go. A big operation like ours could never get away without spraying. Even the carrot field," he said, indicating the field to the west, "isn't doing as well now as it would be if I'd been able to spray ... ah ... more."

"Mechanical cultivation pays off in other ways. It improves aeration and slows down erosion. Wait for the drought. You'll be glad you broke up the soil so the water doesn't run off."

"I was reading about organic growing on the net the other day. They make it sound so easy."

"It is a simpler way to do things."

"But Anna, if everyone switched to organic, can you imagine the cost of food? The poorer countries would starve."

"We're not suggesting that we go back to the horse-drawn plow. There are modern organic improvements too."

By now they'd reached the porch off her kitchen. Anna asked Del inside while she went to wash up, but he chose to stay on the deck. "Beautiful view from here."

She nodded in agreement. "It's the mountain. It adds a dimension you don't get from flat land."

A line of fluffy clouds with dark underbellies rode over the mountain, but the sky above shone clear. Now that the crops were established, solid rows radiated from beyond the mown lawn and grape trellises toward the first rise. Anna eyed them critically, searching for spots of paler foliage, weed growth, or missed patches. As always, when she looked across the field she saw chores waiting to be done, as well as potential problems, but she also felt self-satisfied.

She excused herself and hurried to the downstairs half bath. Soon a facecloth was stained with the red earth of her field, and her face tingled from scrubbing. She smeared some moisture cream over it. Even with the liberal amount of sun block she applied every morning, and the baseball cap she habitually wore, she had tanned a deep, golden brown, and her hair had lightened from the sun. She yanked the elastic holding the ponytail, tugged a brush through the dry strands, then divided it into threes to fashion a fat braid that fell down her back.

Anna didn't usually care about her appearance, but now she wished she'd taken the time to condition her hair and to wear gloves as she worked. It occurred to her that she was primping for Del VanOrthrum. Should she be worried? Probably.

Two highways ran the length of the Valley. The secondary one sprouted commercial sections wherever the rural roads intersected with it: farm markets and grocery stores, gas stations and muffler shops, video stores and fast-food restaurants. Beyond these busy little hubs were housing subdivisions and schools, and after that farms and forests; then, on either side of the long Valley, the green-blue of North and South Mountains. It only took fifteen minutes for Del and Anna to drive from her farm to one of the fast-food joints where the dust on Anna's knees wouldn't be noticed.

"Coffee is one of my vices," Anna admitted. "I drink far too much of it."

"What the heck," Del replied. "Better than booze or cigarettes."

He held the heavy glass door open with one hand and placed his palm on the small of her back to guide her through. It felt so right there, the physical connection, as if it made them emotionally closer too.

"Did you ever smoke?" she asked.

"When I was in my late teens. Thought it made me look older. How about you?"

She shook her head. "I played a lot of sports in those days. Didn't want to do anything to affect my breathing."

They stood side by side, looking up at the printed list. "Not exactly the menu I envisioned for our first date."

Their first date? Anna glanced at his profile. He didn't seem to think there was anything strange about what he'd just said. She, on the other hand, felt charged with an anticipation that both frightened and excited her.

The clerk behind the counter asked, "What'll you have?"

Del ordered a huge meal with a bacon burger, fries, onion rings, and a chocolate milkshake. Anna settled on a chicken burger with a coffee. As they carried their trays toward a window seat, Del saw a man he knew and paused to say a few words. Anna continued walking, trying to pretend she didn't notice so he wouldn't have to go through the uncomfortable act of introducing her.

"Anna," Del said, stopping her. "Have you met Peter Yetman?"

"Hello," she said, feeling awkward.

Del continued his introduction. "Anna owns a farm over in Havenville."

Peter nodded. "I know a woman who buys eggs from you. Karen Smyth? She's a good friend of my wife's."

Anna felt Del stiffen at her side. "Yes, Karen and her mother both stop by."

"Are organic eggs really that much better?" Peter asked.

"I think the appeal is really the dark colored yolks," Anna explained. "That comes from the variety of food my hens get. They eat a lot more than commercial feed."

"She means bugs," Del said jokingly. "Her hens are free-range."

"I'm going to have to give them a try," Peter said. "Do you ever sell in large lots? I have a bakery and restaurant over in Beachville."

"That lovely place right on the water?" He nodded. "Everything I've ever tasted from there is delicious."

Del asked, "How many eggs do you buy a week, Peter?"

"Are you her agent or something?" Peter teased.

"Just thinking we could bring some flats over on Saturday. Right, Anna?"

She smiled at him. Was that to be their second date? Or was he just trying to drum up more business for her? "Sure."

When they finally took their own seats, Del said, "I hope you don't mind me doing that?"

"No . . . no, it was thoughtful of you."

"Then why do you look so worried?"

Anna chuckled. "I've never had a single order that large before. It will be two days worth of production. I'm going to have to take down the sale sign on Thursday. I can keep them in my kitchen fridge but that means I have to clean the other food out." She laughed. "Housework isn't my forte."

"You've got the tidiest barn I've ever seen."

"Thanks. I do like to be organized out there."

"Even though I live by myself, I have a cleaning service in twice a week. Otherwise my dirty socks take on a life of their own." He marched his fingers across the tabletop.

"Do you have a house?"

"In Toronto? No, just an apartment. Two bedrooms, one I use as my office. It just seems easier that way. I've never wanted to mow grass on Sundays, or shovel out a driveway, if you know what I mean."

It sounded as if he had no interest in being domestic or in ever marrying. "Houses are more work, that's for sure."

"What do you do with your truck in the winter? Do you have a garage?"

"On the far side of the barn."

He grimaced. "Do you hire someone to shovel for you?"

"No. As a matter of fact, I make a few bucks plowing snow around Havenville. The last couple of winters have been so mild, there hasn't been much snow to worry about." Anna took a bite of her burger. The lack of snow—and accompanying lack of income—was one of the reasons for her money problems.

"You're amazing. I hope you know that. The amount of work you accomplish in the average day would cripple most people."

"I worked up to it, believe me. Besides, you're a farmer now too. You work hard."

"Mike sees that I get the easy jobs." He flexed his muscles. "Nevertheless, my fellow teachers aren't going to recognize me."

"Do you miss the city?"

"Not as much as I thought I would. Thought I'd be lonely and bored, but I'm usually too tuckered out to think of anything but food and sleep when I get in."

"I know what you mean."

"Another thing that's surprising me is that I like the work. I like being outside all day. I like being able to see the sky every time I raise my head."

"Very different from Toronto."

"Don't get me wrong. I like my job there too, and that's where my friends are. This is like a holiday for me in that it's so different."

"A change is as good as a rest." Once again, Anna concentrated on her lunch. She didn't like to think of Del leaving the Valley come September. Not at all.

After taking a sip of his milkshake, Del said, "I suppose you'll want to get some chores done before we drive over to the coast on Saturday? Would eleven in the morning give you enough time?"

She nodded. The food in her mouth suddenly

seemed too dry to swallow. Del was watching her, studying her. It was if he knew she felt flustered. A slow smile spread across his face.

"Let's make a day of it," he said. "Eat brunch, walk along the beach."

Was he flirting with her? Yes. Anna gulped. She didn't know how to do that anymore. If a quick bite in a fast-food joint was beyond her social skills, how would she ever cope on Saturday?

Chapter Nine

"Will you look at that," Diana said with a sigh.

Anna joined her friend at the railing and gazed northwest where the mountain stood silhouetted against a sky shot with purple and orange clouds. A gentle breeze washed over her face and throat, drying the glow of moisture that had formed from leaning over the hot coals. Behind them the chicken sizzled on the barbeque.

The two women had met four years earlier when Diana started manning the cash in the grocery and gas station a mile down the road. Her husband, Sol, worked on the oil rigs off Newfoundland and was often away. It seemed inevitable that the two lonely women, both in their early twenties at the time, should form a friend-ship.

"Do you want to eat out here or inside?" Anna asked.

"This is really lovely." Diana slapped her bare arm. "But the mosquitoes have found us."

"Wish the bats would eat them. I built a bat house, but I don't think they've moved in yet."

"Sol thinks you should hang a bug light over the chicken runs."

"Frittered bug. Yum," Anna replied dryly. "I don't like that zapping, sizzling noise they make."

Diana chuckled and pushed herself off the railing. "I'll finish putting the salad together."

Anna turned back to the meat. "Thanks. This is pretty much done. Should we go wild and open that bottle of wine that's been in the fridge all spring?"

"Absolutely. We've got to celebrate you getting a boyfriend. Finally."

"He's not a boyfriend. We haven't even had a real date yet. I don't even know if he wants to date me."

"Yeah, yeah. I'm sure you have all sorts of reservations about the man. Come in and rhyme them off to me."

Once Diana disappeared inside, the porch light snapped on. Almost immediately two moths fluttered up toward the bulb. It wouldn't singe their wings yet, not until it heated up, but the inevitable loomed.

Anna used the tongs to lift the meat onto a clean plate, turned off the gas, and lowered the barbeque cover. As soon as she closed the kitchen door behind her, she switched off the porch light.

"That smells heavenly," Anna said, leaning over the salad bowl to better breathe in the garlic and vinegar aroma.

Diana returned from the refrigerator with a tray of fresh Parmesan. "No one could accuse this of being a diet salad," she said, spooning the cheese over the greens, "not with all that bacon and oil and croutons."

"Yummy. I'm starving."

"Of course you are. Imagine not eating until this late every night. No wonder you're getting so skinny."

Anna shook the loose waistband on her pants. "I have lost a lot of weight. None of my clothes fit."

"What are you going to wear tomorrow?"

"Jeans?"

"Wouldn't you like to wear a dress for a change?"

"To deliver eggs?"

Diana rammed her hands on her ample hips.

"Has the man ever seen you in anything other than jeans?"

"No, but I had on my yellow blouse at the Vegetable Growers meeting. Besides, Diana, I'm not out to impress Del."

"Do yourself a favor. Dress up for once in your life."

"Even if I have a dress that still fits me, I can't wear it. My legs are so white they're practically blue."

"How can you work outdoors all day and not have tanned legs?"

"It would be impractical to wear shorts; I spend a lot of time crawling around on the ground."

"Were you a tomboy as a kid?"

"Strangely, no."

Diana chuckled. "Should we light the candles?"

"Sure."

The two friends sat opposite each other at the long dining room table eating their chicken and salads and sipping chilled white wine. Anna could tell, by the way Diana kept up a disjointed conversation about inconsequential things, that she had something on her mind.

"Anna, I don't think you should go out with Del VanOrthrum," she said with exaggerated seriousness.

Anna dropped her fork onto her plate with a clatter. "What! You've been after me for years to get into dating."

"That was before."

"Before what?"

Diana laid down her knife and fork, dabbed her mouth, and said solemnly, "Before you got all dowdy and old. No man could want you now. You'll just get your heart broken if you try."

Anna threw a roll at her. She knew she was physically attractive, if a bit too skinny. Of course, her hands looked like alligator backs and she would likely wrinkle young because of all the time she spent in the sun. Even so, it wasn't her physical self that turned people away; it was her personality.

"I know I'm a bit unapproachable."

"Unapproachable?" Diana scoffed. "If a man gives you the least bit of attention, you bite his head off."

"There's an insect that does that, isn't there? Is it the praying mantis?"

"Don't try to change the topic. What have you done differently around Del? Or is he just a glutton for punishment?"

"Nothing," Anna lied. "Have you heard from Sol this week?"

Diana ignored her question. "You must have done something. Think."

Anna took a sip of wine. Diana was right; Del had seen a different side of her personality. She whispered, "I cried," and took a fork of salad.

"Pardon?"

Diana waited, her glass half-raised to her mouth, while Anna finished swallowing. "When Ricky got hurt, I cried."

"Ah . . . you let down your guard, and he saw your softer side."

"He caught me at a bad time, that's all."

"He saw you at your worst, and he still wants you."

A jolt of alarm shot through her. "He doesn't *want* me. He's just . . . we're friends, like his father and I are friends."

"It could turn into more."

"I don't want it to turn into more." Anna realized she'd raised her voice.

"Why not? By all accounts he's a nice, good-looking, respectable man."

"He's going back to Toronto in September."

"Oh, Anna," Diana said, looking disappointed in her. "Are you only going out with him because you know it can't lead anywhere?"

"I'm not going out with him, I told you. And even if I were . . . sure, I am glad it can't be long-term. That takes the pressure off both of us."

"Girlfriend, are you ever going to get over that rat, Chris Parker?"

"I'm over him."

"Over what happened five years ago?"

Now Anna felt exasperated. "Can we drop it? Please?"

"Well, just be nice when you're with Del."

"I'm nice," Anna snapped. "Why do you think I'm not nice?"

Diana smiled and pointed the tines of her fork at Anna. "If you call throwing little hissy-fits like the one you're having right now nice, then no wonder you don't have a boyfriend."

Diana meant well, Anna knew, but she just didn't understand. Not every woman needed a man to make her whole. Anna learned years earlier that she didn't have what it took to maintain a serious relationship. She wasn't sensitive enough to other people's feelings while, at the same time, she was too sensitive of her own feelings. On the whole, she was much better off living alone. Once she sorted out her financial difficulties and got the farm under control, she would be completely happy.

The next morning, after doing the chores and washing the latest eggs, Anna donned a clean pair of cotton trousers, which she cinched up with a belt, and a sleeveless cotton sweater. She considered foregoing the hat, but one look in the mirror had her changing her mind. Her tall forehead looked white compared to her tanned cheeks. All her baseball caps were grimy. She almost panicked until she found a straw hat that had been on her closet shelf since she moved to Havenville. It looked jaunty on her head, but the silk flower on its brim almost screamed cutesy-pie.

After loading the flats of eggs from the refrigerators onto a trolley, she rolled them down to the barn. The metal floor on the back of her truck looked hard and slippery. If she started to get more of these large orders, she'd need to build some kind of braced shelving and buy boxes to carry them. What could she use in the meantime? She left the trolley and went into the barn.

This, the upper level of the barn, had wide plank floors that had worn smooth, and were slightly indented where countless feet had trod on them over the previous century. The dark, rough wooden walls had never, in all their years of existence, seen a coat of paint. A grid of fat beams, fitted into one another with clever notches and held together with wooden dowels, supported the arched roof. Half of this floor had been divided into enough stalls to house a dozen horses. Except for a few months one year when a neighbor temporarily used the stalls until he replaced his own barn, which had burned down, they'd been empty since she bought the place. There was a loft above the stalls, but Anna hadn't been up there in years either.

Once her eyes adjusted to the dim light, Anna looked around. The empty feed bags might be enough cushion to protect the eggs. She stood with either foot braced on a sawhorse to reach the bags where they were draped over a beam. A shower of dirt and cobwebs had her squinting her eyes as she tossed the sacks onto the floor behind her. The air swirled with nutty-smelling dust. By the time she had a dozen sacks wrestled back out into the sunshine, her nice clean trousers were streaked with grime and the straw hat had disappeared.

"Morning."

Anna dropped the bags and slapped the dust from her hands. "Hi, Del."

She was admiring the way his shoulders moved as he worked so it took a moment to realize what he was actually doing.

"Hope you don't mind?" he asked. "I thought we'd go in our farm truck. Okay with you?"

Del already had half of the flats loaded into square egg boxes and was stacking them in the back of his fancy truck. Here she was, supposedly the professional poultry person, and he had the egg boxes. She felt her face color and she clenched her fists.

"How did you know I wouldn't have the right boxes?"

He frowned. "I didn't. I saw these as I was leaving and figured they'd be more use to you than us." He paused, then added unnecessarily, "We don't have chickens."

Anna realized she was irritated at herself, not at Del, but she couldn't seem to smile. "I'll just go wash up again."

I am so prickly, she fumed, marching back to the house. *Now he not only believes I'm incapable of running my own business, but he thinks me rude and ungrateful. He's going to have a miserable time and it will be all my fault. I might as well just tell him to leave right now, before I really get hurt.*

Chapter Ten

Del didn't regret his impulse to bring the egg boxes that morning; Anna needed them. He'd known the instant he saw her stepping into the sunlight with the feedbags in her arms that she'd feel embarrassed. Sure enough, the color crept up her throat, and her face became that careful, if beautiful, mask he'd come to know so well. The poor woman expected too much of herself.

He figured that some people, when they got nervous, embarrassed, or frightened, turned boisterous. Others giggled. A lot of people, especially men, threw temper tantrums. Anna's defense mechanism was to get cold and hard. Del shook his head. The more Anna tried to appear indifferent, the easier it was for him to see that she cared a great deal. He'd never met such a complex, interesting woman before. She so intrigued him, he couldn't go twenty minutes without thinking about her. She even interfered with his sleep.

Del finished loading the eggs onto his truck, then he scooped up the empty feedbags and carried them back into the barn. The cavernous size surprised him. A snowplow blade was pushed into one corner, with an old-fashioned disk plow beside that. Each of them looked clean and sharpened. A tidy stack of woodchip bales lined the east wall. His whole apartment in Toronto could fit on the wide, open floor that remained. It would be a great spot for a party; he envisioned a line of people sitting up on the loft with their arms braced on the railing and their feet wiggling to the music.

He chuckled. That country music that Mike and Stubby forced on him must be getting under his skin.

He dropped the feedbags over a couple of sawhorses and almost stepped on a straw hat. It was a delicate, feminine thing with a yellow ribbon wound along the brim. He wiped his hands on his jeans before scooping it off the floor.

Anna waited for him out beside the truck. She'd changed into blue jeans and a loose T-shirt. Her hair was yanked in a high and tight ponytail that left her throat looking long and regal.

"You want this?" he said, handing her the straw hat. She demurred so he carefully placed it on her head. Her eyes were huge and worried. He took her hand and pulled it up so he could kiss her knuckles.

"You'd look beautiful with one of those feed sacks wrapped around your head, turban-style."

"You don't like this hat?"

"Sure I do," he said, adjusting the angle. "It looks jaunty. But I like you in a baseball cap just as much."

She smiled at that. Still holding hands, they walked together to his truck.

Anna cleared her throat and said, "Thank you for loading the eggs."

"No problem." He opened the door on the passenger side and gave her a hand up.

It had been so long since Del was in Beachville that Anna had to give him directions. For ten minutes, they drove past potato fields and orchards, then turned and zigzagged up the side of North Mountain, past rocky fields where the grass was sheared short by grazing cows. Then the mountain leveled to a plateau that gently sloped down to the Bay of Fundy.

Beachville had changed since he was a boy. The wild stretch of gravel beach was still there but now, rather than butting up against windblown trees and thick shrubs, a row of summer cottages faced the water. He couldn't blame people for building there, on this beautiful coast, but something had been lost nevertheless.

The wharf had grown from a rickety wooden structure to a long, cement-and-stone jetty. Below it, a couple of Cape Islander fishing boats lay on their keels in the mud like beached whales. The Bay of Fundy has the highest tides in the world. It would take a behemoth structure to reach deep enough into the bay so that boats would still be floating in water when the tide dropped forty feet every twelve and a half hours.

Del backed up to what appeared to be the kitchen entrance of Peter's Restaurant and Bakery. The moment he opened his door he could smell an exotic combination of briny ocean water and rising yeast bread.

Anna was already undoing the restraining straps on the back of the truck. She'd relaxed considerably during the drive over, and he didn't want to horn in on her business transaction, so he asked, "Do you want me to give you a hand with those?"

"No thanks. Why don't you go inside and order us a brunch."

"Okay. You like your coffee black, right?"

She smiled at him. "Right. Would you order

me that egg-and-ham dish, the one with the hollandaise sauce?"

"Oh yeah, that's what I'm going to have too," he said, realizing he was starving.

It felt strange and ungentlemanly to turn his back and leave her with the heavy job of carrying the eggs inside. Should he go through the kitchen door so he could at least tell Peter that they'd arrived? He compromised by ringing the delivery bell before heading around the gravel parking lot to the main entrance.

The interior of the restaurant looked as if it had been decorated by the Women's Institute: ruffled curtains, dried flower arrangements in the center of each round table, and cushions tied to the seats of the wooden chairs. Del felt clumsy and too big as he maneuvered to the last empty table by the plate-glass window. He hadn't realized how popular this brunch was. Except for two white-haired men, all the tables were occupied by women. They smiled at him from every corner.

The waitress wore a frilly apron that matched the curtains. Del placed the order. Then he shifted his chair so his legs weren't cramped under the table. That's when he saw, through the gap in the curtains, Karen Smyth and another woman walking toward the restaurant. His chair scraped and banged as he moved it again, this time so he faced away from the door. He didn't want to talk to Karen Smyth. Every time he thought about the way she had implied that his father and Anna were dating, his teeth ground.

For five minutes, Del sipped his coffee and watched the kitchen door. He pictured Anna in there, chatting with the kitchen crew, and collecting a nice check for her eggs. When she did appear, Peter, wearing a white cook's hat over his hair, walked by her side. He held a big metal bowl in his hands. The two of them looked deep in conversation.

"Peter! Hello!" Karen Smyth called from her table.

"Hi girls," Peter said. A few strides took him to Karen's side. "Look at this, will you?" Peter tilted his bowl so the woman Karen was with could see inside. "Did you ever see yolks so dark before?"

Del couldn't hear Karen's reply, but he saw the nasty look on her face as she spied Anna. A surge of protective feelings brought him to his feet.

"I don't buy from her anymore," Karen said loudly. "The last time I bought her eggs, one of them was rotten and I had to throw the whole flat out. Can't be too careful."

"If you had a rotten egg, Karen," Del said, bumping into a woman's chair in his rush to reach Anna, "it didn't come from Anna Mac-Frail. I've seen how she handles her produce; no one could take better care than she does."

"Del!" Karen looked stricken.

"Or maybe you got them mixed up with some old ones you had around." Del tried to keep his voice calm, but he glared at Karen. She knew perfectly well that she could further ruin Anna's business by blabbing that kind of nonsense here in a crowded restaurant.

Karen sniffed. "Anything's possible."

Del put his arm across Anna's shoulders. She smiled at him but her body was stiff and unyielding.

After an awkward moment, Peter said, "Well, if the color of these yolks is any indication of nutrition, these eggs are packed with health. How do you get them to look like this?"

"I plant leaf lettuce—organic leaf lettuce—for them. The girls really love the stuff."

Grinning, Peter headed back toward the kitchen. "She calls them 'the girls.' No wonder the eggs are so huge; her chickens are pampered."

Neither Del nor Anna mentioned Karen while they ate their brunch. Anna still looked uncomfortable, cutting her muffin into little slices and rolling the handle of her knife around the placemat, so he kept up a running commentary about how Beachville had changed.

"When I was a kid, my father used to collect agate and amethyst along the shore further down the coast. One time he parked the car right on the beach and we headed off with our buckets. Gosh, I suppose I must have been about seven years old. Luckily, my mother stayed in the car because we were way down on a point when the tide started to come in. She blew the horn for all she was worth and moved the car. When we saw the water coming, we threw those buckets and ran like the dickens." He laughed at the memory and was awarded by an amused smile on Anna's face. "Even so, I had to ride on my dad's shoulder the last bit because the water was up to his waist."

"Your father has told me about your mom. He really loved her."

"Oh yeah, those two. . . . I'm sure they went through their rough spots like other married couples, but they were pretty much a team."

"Did she work in the fields?"

"No, no. The house was her domain. Heaven help you if you tried to change something in her kitchen."

Anna had a far-away look in her eyes, so he asked, "What were your parents like?"

"Both my folks were in the civil service.

Middle-management, nothing fancy, but they made a comfortable living. After they died I used to wonder if they were saving up their energies for retirement. They lived such staid lives, never took risks, never traveled or had exotic hobbies. The fact that I wanted to go to agricultural college shocked them." She chuckled. "I had to couch it in terms they could understand. They had been civil servants all their working lives, so I told them that I wanted to work in a government department: Agriculture Canada."

"You didn't want a cushy government job?"

"No, I wanted to work on a farm."

"But you lived in Ottawa. A city."

"I had a friend who owned a horse that was stabled north of the city and I used to go with her on weekends—an hour on the bus, mind you. I loved the smell of the barn, and the feel of standing in a big, open field with all that sky."

"Are you ever going to buy a horse of your own?"

"No," she said emphatically. "A horse would make me feel guilty all the time, as if I should be riding it, or grooming it, or paying attention to it. Ricky is enough pet for me."

When they left the restaurant, they headed down over the bluff toward the beach. A cool breeze wafted off the water, carrying with it the tang of salt and the hoarse cry of seagulls. The beach seemed divided into bands, the slimy bedrock closer to the water, then bigger boulders that gave way to smaller rocks, ending with tiny pebbles that eons of ocean pounding had rounded like granite marbles. It crunched and rolled underfoot making the walking an effort. Del took Anna's hand.

"Thank you for sticking up for me in there," Anna said.

"That Karen Smyth. What a nasty piece of work she is."

"I thought she was one of the few people around here who liked me." She looked at him with a frown. "I wonder if she's jealous. I mean . . . if she thinks we're going out together. She phoned me one night and asked if you were with me."

"I'm sorry, Anna. That was probably the day I saw her at your house. She was under the mistaken impression that I was going to her house for supper."

Anna smiled. "She said you stood her up."

"I'm sorry if I cost you a customer."

She shrugged. "A flat every other week isn't going to make any difference. And what you did in there will probably get me a customer or two."

"What would you have said if I hadn't been there?"

She kicked a small rock and it rattled down toward the water. "I'm not sure. . . ."

Once again Del had a feeling that he was missing a subtext. It probably had something to do with what Donald Parker had told him; how he accused Anna of being sneaky. Was Karen involved in that incident? Karen and Peggy Parker, Donald's daughter, were around the same age. Maybe Karen was there at the Parker house when they had the big blow-up, or whatever it was.

He stopped and pulled Anna around to face him. "You've got to stick up for yourself. You can't let people like Karen and that jerk, Donald Parker, get away with lying about you."

She swiped a strand of hair off her face, but she didn't let go of his hand. "I know."

"And another thing, while I'm in the mood to lecture you. We are going out together. We're dating. Is that a problem with you?"

She put the flat of her hand on his chest. "I'd like that, if you're sure?"

He could feel the heat of her hand through his shirt. "Of course I'm sure."

She looked hopeful, but a little sad, as if she didn't believe things would work out. He cupped his free hand on the back of her neck and kissed her. The instant their lips met, he was awash with sensations, as if he'd been waiting all his adult life for this feeling. He felt heady and tender and totally aware of Anna, connected to her on many levels. Her lips were warm and tasted salty, probably from the ocean spray. It thrilled Del right to the marrow that Anna kissed him back.

Chapter Eleven

Even after a half-dozen dates, Anna still felt uncomfortable going out in public with Del. Invariably, they ran into someone one or the other of them knew. She hated the idea that the gossip about her might reflect poorly on Del. He was such a good man.

"You're a million miles away," Del said as they pulled into the parking space behind the restaurant.

"Woolgathering," she apologized.

The parking lot had been carved out of the side of a steep hill. The trees still standing on the top were alive with crows squawking and cawing, wings fluttering, leaves shaking. Above them, the shimmering blue of the early night spread across the sky.

Del craned his neck and looked up at the crows. "Kind of like that Hitchcock movie, *The Birds*," he said.

"Funny, but rather than scaring me, the sight of all these birds gives me a little thrill."

Del took her hand and they started toward the restaurant's back entrance. "I know what you mean. It's exciting."

"I also like the idea that they get to be with one another overnight. That they're social creatures."

They stepped over cobblestones and under an ivy-draped arch. Most of the round tables in the courtyard were already occupied, but they found a small one in the corner next to a bubbling miniature fountain. An oily cooking smell flowed from an air vent.

Anna kept her eyes on Del or the floor, so she didn't know if anyone was watching them. Suddenly, she drew herself up. Del didn't care that people knew they were seeing one another, so why should she. Yes, thanks to Donald Parker, she did have a bad reputation. But what he told people wasn't the truth. She didn't lie and she found it hard to believe she broke his son's heart. Chris was the one who took off, not her.

As far as Anna knew, the one thing she *was* guilty of, Donald never spoke about to anyone.

"I don't think the crows flocked like this when I was a kid," Del said, continuing the conversation.

"I remember the first time I noticed them. I was just packing up my tools for the day."

"Dusk," Del interrupted. "They always head off toward town at dusk."

"That's right. It went on for ten minutes or more, all of them headed southeast, toward here, I guess."

The waitress arrived. Anna wanted a spinach salad but she knew that the greens wouldn't be local. The Valley spinach would have bolted by now, with all the heat. So she ordered a Caesar salad with a side of garlic bread. Del, true to form, chose a fat steak with fries. The waitress quickly returned with a beer for Del and a cappuccino for Anna.

"Do you suppose the crow families find one another and roost on the same branch?" Del asked, once the waitress had left.

Anna licked the cappuccino foam off her lip. "I've never heard that."

"I don't know if it's my age, or my grandmother getting sick, but this summer I've developed a new appreciation for family."

"Oh?"

"I told you I have a sister?"

Anna's throat tightened so she just nodded. She knew of Del's sister. Maureen VanOrthrum was the Parkers' lawyer five years earlier. Anna had never met Maureen, but she'd had dealings with her indirectly through her own lawyer.

"Maureen has two kids: Ken and Hanna. The rugrats."

"I take it they're young?"

He frowned. "I guess I should stop calling them rugrats, now that they're going to school. Ken is eight, and Hanna's five." He snickered. "Anyway, I'm getting to know them. It's not that I didn't know them before. I visit a couple of times a year."

As Del talked about his niece and nephew, Anna watched his face. Clearly, he loved those children. He'd probably have children of his own some day. They'd be so very beautiful. Anna felt a stab of jealousy. The woman Del married would be very lucky indeed.

"The other day I went down to Maureen's for supper," he said. "There's a fence around her backyard, and an apple tree just inside the gate. I no sooner stepped in when—*bang!*" He hunched over with a pained look on his face. "Those two jumped out of the tree and landed on me. An ambush! We must have wrestled for twenty minutes."

Anna had to chuckle, he looked so cute telling the story. She would love to wrestle with him on a back lawn, under an apple tree.

"It's going to be really hard to go back to Toronto," he said, "and leave those kids. I love them." He sobered.

When he didn't speak for a moment, Anna searched for something to say. "You'll still visit."

He shrugged. "I never really realized what blood means. Those kids are *family*. If anyone tried to harm them, I'd go nuts."

"Yes . . . well . . ." Anna stammered.

Maureen, Del's sister, would never want her as part of their family. She had represented the Parkers in court five years earlier. Donald and Marge claimed that they took Anna into their family and she turned on them. Family members didn't do that to one another. Suddenly, as the memories assailed Anna, she shuddered and hid her fists under the table.

Del looked concerned. "Anna?"

"I'm starving," Anna said, struggling to keep her voice level. "Where is that waitress?"

"What's wrong?"

She managed a one-shouldered shrug, then motioned toward the glass chimney between them. "Would you light those candles please, Del?"

"You shivered. Are you warm enough? Want to move to a table inside?"

"No, it's such a lovely night."

Del didn't have a match so he motioned to a waiter. By the time the candle had been lit, Anna had herself better in hand.

"Maybe you and I should go to Maureen's for supper one night?" Del suggested. "You can see the terrible twosome for yourself."

Anna made a noncommittal sound and picked up her mug. She couldn't go to Maureen's house. She strongly doubted that she'd ever be invited, considering what Del's sister knew about her.

On the other hand, five years had passed since the trial. Perhaps Maureen had so many clients that she wouldn't remember the details. Anna herself hadn't made an appearance in court. She was probably just a dim name on an affidavit to Maureen. She started to feel better.

"I'd love to meet your niece and nephew someday, Del."

The waitress appeared with their food. While they ate, the conversation moved onto other topics. Anna relaxed and forgot all about the impediments to her relationship with Del VanOrthrum. Instead she concentrated on savoring the little time she did have to be with him.

Chapter Twelve

Anna slipped another elastic from the band around her left wrist and looped it over the ends of the rubbery-feeling leaves she'd gathered in her right hand. Then she shuffled along to the next plant. She and her friend, Diana, slowly worked their way up the field lifting cauliflower leaves to shade the developing vegetables. If direct sunlight hit her precious cauliflower curds, they'd turn brown and get strong-tasting. She wanted them to grow heavy and fat with surfaces that looked like fluffy white clouds.

She worked by rote because her mind was on Del, specifically on the way he looked at her with that little secret smile that she could read even in a crowded restaurant. The previous few weeks they'd spent so much time together, or talking on the phone, that she found herself telling him tiny, almost insignificant things about her day. She wanted to hear about his day too, everything. He told her how Stubby made coffee that tasted like spent tractor oil, and that Del himself had worn out the seat of another pair of jeans.

"Why, oh why did you choose to grow cauliflower?" Diana complained, her voice bringing Anna came back to the present.

"A number of reasons. I canvassed the warehouses last fall and they said they'd buy them from me, not that I can sell them as organic now, and—"

"Anna."

"I thought I could do the labor myself, and—"

"Anna! It was a rhetorical question."

Diana was a willing worker, and Anna didn't begrudge the money she paid her, but her friend wasn't built to do farm labor. While Anna tied the plants on either side of the row she moved along, Diana only did one side.

"I'm sick of cauliflower and I haven't even had one this season. And we're going to stink of this stuff for days."

"Grumble, grumble." The cauliflowers themselves didn't smell, but the field had a rotting vegetation aroma reminiscent of boiling cabbage.

Diana groaned as she straightened her back. "Where did you and Del go last night?"

"Just to his place. We rented a movie and picked up a pizza."

"Oh yeah? What's his place like?"

"You've seen it from the outside." She knew that Diana had driven by because the big white house and buildings of Suffenbrook Farms stood out, so much so that people used it as a landmark. "The inside matches. It's big and airy and white. Very nice. They've got one of those restaurant-sized stoves with two ovens and eight burners."

"Whatever for?"

"Del's mother used to cook big meals for all the employees in the old days, before the big field equipment."

"Bet he has a machine that'll do this job," Diana grumbled.

"No, as far as I know this still has to be done by hand." That was another reason Anna had decided to grow cauliflower. The big operations couldn't do this job mechanically any more than she could, so they didn't have an advantage with their huge farm equipment.

"What's the rest of the house like?"

"Clean, bright. It's been a man's house for a lot of years."

"Oh, Anna, needs a woman's touch, eh? You volunteering?"

"No! I told you, Del's moving back to Toronto in a few weeks."

Anna felt Diana's eyes on her, but she didn't rise to the bait. "The den's nice. That's where we watched the movie. Leather furniture with hand-woven throws. A big hunting print on the wall. There's a gorgeous stone fireplace that must be cozy in the winter."

She'd likely never get to sit before a fire in that room, unless Del came home for a visit on holidays during the school term. She wasn't even confident that he intended to continue their relationship once he left. Oh, Del was kind and considerate and funny, but he'd never indicated that she was anything other than a summer fling. She vowed to herself that she'd enjoy every minute she had with him because, if he didn't come back to her, those memories would have to last her the rest of her life.

"Hey," Diana exclaimed. "Look who's coming."

Ricky trotted up the row toward Anna. She still favored her damaged leg, but, like all cats, she had healed quickly. When the fur grew all the way back in, she'd look as if she'd never had the operation at all.

"Oh sure," Diana grumbled good-naturedly. "You'll stop work to cuddle a cat."

Ricky pressed her head against Anna's neck. "This is the farthest she's been since she got mauled. I think she's afraid to be out alone now."

"Can you blame her?"

"No." She scooped the cat up and nuzzled in the dusty fur at her neck. "Once bitten, twice shy."

Once bitten, twice shy . . . for the second time in her life, Anna had fallen in love, and it terrified her. She struggled with the fear every day, even though Del was nothing like Chris. For one thing, he made no promises to her. More importantly, Anna made no promises to herself. Every morning she looked in the mirror, determined to be thankful for what she'd been given and not hope for more. It was a painful exercise, like pulling off a bandage. If she let herself believe they had a future together, if she allowed her heart to get infected with that hope, she would die when he left.

Diana groaned. "That's it. I need a break."

They were almost to the end of a row, but Anna knew better than to work Diana too hard, especially this early in the job. As it was, she was bound to be stiff by the next morning.

"It's almost lunchtime anyway." Anna lowered her arms so Ricky would jump out, but the cat leaned back, determined to hang on, so she draped her over her shoulder.

"Give me your knife, Anna." Diana leaned over a plant. "I want to take this one home."

"I thought you were sick of cauliflower." She dug her penknife from her back pocket.

"It's so cute."

Diana pushed the leaves aside, exposing a head that had already turned white even though it was only a few inches across. She grunted as she sawed through the stalk and sliced off the leaves. "How do you do this day in and day out?"

"You get used to it."

Anna looked east, toward the potatoes. Their color was off. "Would you go down and put the kettle on, please Diana? I'll be there in a second."

Diana wiped the blade of the knife on the side of her jeans, closed it, and handed it back to Anna. "I'd rather have a beer."

"I don't have any. But there's ice tea in the fridge."

Even if she did have cold beer, Anna wouldn't want Diana to drink it. Alcohol didn't mix well with fieldwork. At least they didn't have the hot sun pounding down on their backs; the sky was white with high cloud cover.

Ricky still draped over her shoulder as Anna walked the few paces up to the end of the field, then across toward the potatoes. Irrigation pipes still lay where she'd dragged them the previous week. She glanced down to gauge a step over one of them. Something moved. She looked closer. Two, three, five beetles with black-and-yellow striped shells marched relentlessly across the packed dirt. Oh no. The Colorado potato beetle had found her. She speed-walked toward the plants. It had only been a few days since she last checked here and she had thought herself lucky then, but this infestation made up for lost time.

Virtually every leaf in sight had circular wounds where they'd been eaten away.

She pried Ricky off her shoulder and started plucking the bugs off with her bare hands. Pick, drop, stomp. Pick, drop, stomp.

Anna had put in an area the size of half a football field full of potato plants. It would take her days to get to every plant—assuming there were any leaves left by then. Pick, pick, drop, stomp. Pick, pick, pick, drop, stomp.

Her heart thudded. She wouldn't lose this entire crop. She couldn't. If she didn't make a profit this fall, she'd lose the farm. She worked feverously, shoving the thigh-high plants apart and searching for the bugs. Some of the leaves had clusters of bright orange eggs stuck to their undersides. Anna snapped off these leaves and ground them into the dirt. Pick, pick, pick, pick . . . both hands flew.

The dinner bell clanged. Diana's hollered words sounded faint over the field. "Anna? Anna! Lunch is ready."

"I can't!" Her voice sounded choked. "Go ahead."

She checked to see how far she'd traveled. Ten feet . . . only ten feet out of thousands. She would work all night. No, she'd hire a crew. Oh, if only she had money in the bank. Pick, pick, pick. . . . Twenty minutes passed.

"Anna! Anna?" Diana walked up the field. "I thought you were coming in for lunch."

"Oh, look . . . look. They're infested."

"Ew, you're using your fingers. Want me to get you some gloves?"

"They'd slow me down."

"Is it just here? On this end of the field?"

Anna felt a flicker of hope, but it quickly died. Once the Colorado potato beetle found a potato field, it swarmed in the millions. It was as if they could call to one another, or could smell potato plants.

Diana sounded concerned. "I'll go check, shall I?"

"Yes, sure." Anna wanted to scream at her to pluck off the bugs, to kill them.

A couple of minutes later, Diana returned. "I don't think it's quite as bad down there."

"Maybe if we concentrate on a section, say this corner of the field, we can save it."

"Oh, Anna, I'm so sorry."

"Please, just pick them off."

"There are too many. Isn't there something you can spray?"

The notion of using a chemical insecticide seemed to be, all at once, both practical and horrific. She believed in organic farming. To fall back on chemicals when the going got rough would be like betraying herself. An angry knot formed in her stomach. There were organic remedies, but she'd never be able to order enough in time.

"Diana, please . . ."

"Do you want me to bring your sandwich up here?" She gingerly leaned over a plant to scoop up a bug in her palm.

"I couldn't eat now."

"Should I get back to the cauliflower?"

Anna took a shaky breath. There wasn't any point in putting that crop in jeopardy, and if Di-

ana was this squeamish, she'd be far too slow
to be any use here. "Yes, please do that."

The afternoon turned into evening. Diana
tried to make Anna go to the house for a meal,
but she'd become a robot who didn't need food.
She did occasionally down mugs of water and,
once, a glass of milk. When the sky started to
color, Anna asked for a flashlight.

"Are you crazy!" Diana screamed. "You've
been at this for eight hours straight. You're not
a machine! Just stop it!"

Her tone brought Anna upright. A burning fa-
tigue stabbed her lower back. "Oh my . . . Diana, I'm so sorry. Look, it's almost dark and
you're still here. Thank you for today. You go
on home."

"I'm not leaving you out here in the field
alone with those disgusting bugs."

"If you could just come back first thing tomorrow?"

"Anna MacFrail! You listen to me right now.
It's time to call it a night. What good will you
do your precious farm if you make yourself
sick?"

"I know that, and I'm going to schedule in
sleep. I just can't waste the evening. How could
I sit in front of the television set when these

things are out here chomping? Every minute counts."

Diana stomped off. As her grumbles faded into the distance, Anna called, "Would you just bring me a flashlight before you go? Please?"

Diana didn't return. Anna worked until the last purple vestiges of the sunset faded. She knew if she stopped, she wouldn't be able to get going again, and yet, she did have to get a flashlight. In this light the plants were masses of black against a gray earth. The air was still and getting moist with dew. She could smell the rotting leaves in the cauliflower patch. Now and again the air moved where a bat flitted above her head.

"I will not let this beat me. I will not fail."

Out on the paved road, a vehicle slowed down. It looked like a tractor with bright lights, high and close together. Beams swung in an arc as it turned onto the drive. She thought that perhaps it was Stubby bringing the tractor around so he could make an early start in the morning. Their carrots were probably ready for the fresh market.

Maybe she could use their tractor's headlights to see by? She found a well of energy and did a slow jog down to the bottom of the field. She had to get to Stubby before he went home.

It was Del who climbed from the cab.

"Oh, I'm so glad to see you," she cried. She checked herself before flying into his arms because she knew she must smell of rot and sweat. "May I borrow your tractor tonight?"

He snickered, relieved. "Here I was afraid you'd be mad at me."

"What do you mean?"

He waved a thumb behind his shoulder. "For bringing this."

With the lack of food and the worry about the potatoes, Anna knew her brain was fuzzy. She didn't think they had a date planned for that evening. "I'd really appreciate it if I could use it tonight. I've got to pick off potato bugs. If I position it right, those headlights will make it almost as good as daytime."

His shoulders slumped. "You really think you can do it by hand?"

"That's how I've done it other years."

"Did you have this many plants?"

"No," she admitted.

"Were there as many bugs?"

She flicked the orange elastics that were still around her wrist from that morning. Why was he trying to discourage her? "Look, I know it's a big job."

"Diana said there were more than she'd ever seen."

He'd been talking to Diana? "Is she still up at the house?"

He shrugged. "She called me."

"Oh?" She snapped the elastics harder. Since when did Diana call Del? The notion that they were talking about her behind her back made her teeth grind.

"I brought the sprayer."

Anna jerked around. She hadn't seen the yellow tank in the gloom behind the tractor. "What do you have inside that thing?" When he told her, Anna cursed. "I can't use that!"

He clutched her on either shoulder. The light was behind and to his side, but it glanced off his eyes making them look shiny and intent. "What's the difference? You told me yourself you can't sell this as organic produce since we over-sprayed."

Yeck, now she could smell the revolting chemical. "That stuff is poison."

"If it was, I wouldn't be using it. They wouldn't be able to sell it for use on food crops. You know that, Anna!"

She jammed her fists on her hips and quoted, "Approximately 504 insects and mite species, nearly 150 plant pathogen species, and 273 weed species are resistant to pesticides." She'd memorized that from the John Deere website.

He dropped his hands. "Do you know how

arrogant you sound? Do you? Millions of people eat treated vegetables every day, with no ill effect. In fact, life expectancy has doubled in the last couple of hundred years. Not all chemicals are bad!"

She crossed her arms over her midriff. "I only use natural products."

He pointed at the sprayer. "And where do you suppose the ingredients for that came from? Outer space? They came from mixing together things found on the earth."

"May I use the headlights or not?"

"You're not going to save the crop without some chemical pest control, Anna. You might as well get that through your thick head."

She swung around on her heel. "I'd rather fail than go against my own conscience."

"Then you will fail."

"Good-bye, Del."

Chapter Thirteen

Del's tractor started up again. Anna watched it turn in a big circle and then head back out toward the paved road. She stood in the blackness and waited for her eyes to get used to the lack of light. The sky was a charcoal gray, too overcast to hope for any moon or stars to see by. She'd get the flashlight herself. Perhaps if she strapped it to her head, she'd still have both hands free.

It was totally dark now, but Anna knew her own land so well that she didn't need a light. She walked down a corridor between grape trellises and rounded the hedge behind the barn. A dark blob detached from the blackness a yard from her feet. She froze. It could be a skunk, or a porcupine. Even a raccoon would be savage if it thought it were protecting its young. After a rustling noise and a faint snorting, the animal disappeared under the hedge.

Anna paused at the end of the chicken runs in the chilling air with the shadows and blackness all around her. A mosquito bit her neck, and dampness seeped through her clothes. A breeze rustled through the hedge and whistled around the corner of the building. Up above a creaking and bumping came from where one of the barn gutters had worked loose. It would be a two-minute job down on the ground, but it wasn't on the ground. She didn't own a ladder tall enough to reach that gutter, and, even if she did, she couldn't maneuver it alone. The gutter would just creak and bang until it fell off and then, when it rained, the water would gush right on top of the hens.

A blanket of helplessness enveloped her. She knew she should go into the barn and find the flashlight, but what was the point? There were too many beetles. Her best efforts wouldn't save those plants. Suddenly a great, hiccupping sob rose from her belly. She worked so hard but even her best wasn't good enough. Now she'd alienated Del. She failed at everything she ever tried.

"*Meow.*"

"Oh, Ricky . . ." Anna drooped and sat on the ground. She pulled the cat into her arms and rocked her back and forth while she tried to get her own crying under control.

The sound of her kitchen door opening made her bring her chin up.

"Anna? Are you out there?"

She sniffed back her tears. "I'm over here."

Diane hurried down the stairs. "My soul, it's dark out here. Where are you?"

Anna climbed to her feet. "Behind the barn."

"Come on, sweetie. Come into the house."

"I . . . I . . ."

"Oh, sweetie," Diane cooed. She gathered Anna in a warm, enveloping hug. "You go ahead and cry."

After a moment, Anna took a couple of bracing breaths and said, "Now I'm going to have a crying headache."

"Come in the house. I kept your dinner warm."

"You're a good friend, Diane."

"No I'm not. I just stayed here so I could eat your food. Nothing for me to go home for with Sol away."

After Anna cleaned up in the bathroom, the two women sat across from each other at the kitchen table. Diane sipped tea while Anna ate. The pork chop, mashed potatoes, and boiled carrots tasted like sawdust, but she dutifully swallowed them.

"So," Diane said, after she poured a mug of tea for Anna. "You turned Del's offer down."

"You saw that, did you?"

"I called him. I know you don't like me to interfere, but I thought you needed help."

"I know you meant well."

"He meant well too."

She sighed heavily. "You'd think, after all the time we've spent together, he'd know I won't use that stuff."

"If you lose the farm, the next owner will probably use it. In the scheme of things, what difference does it make? You can go back to organic next year."

"Diane."

"I know . . . I know you believe it's the morally right thing to do. Your bit to save the planet."

Anna set the knife and fork together on the edge of her plate. "I don't have much. This place is mortgaged to the hilt. And you're my only friend."

"And Del," she interjected.

"I'm not so sure about him after tonight. Besides, he's leaving soon and I'll . . ." Her voice started to crack again so she paused to collect herself. "My point is, if I lose my convictions, what do I have left?"

"Your farm."

"And if I lose it anyway?"

"You have options. You can get a job."

Anna nodded sadly. "I've been emailing that organic farm down in Bridgewater. I could try to work for them next summer. But it's minimum wage, Diane. For four or five months a year."

"So you go on unemployment insurance for the rest of the year like other seasonal laborers."

Anna didn't want to live on government handouts. She didn't want to work for other people; she wanted a farm of her own. She wanted this farm.

A rumbling sound came from outside. "What's that?"

She jumped up and looked out the window. Headlights were turning up the dirt road again. Anna didn't even take the time to put her sneakers back on, she just yanked open the door and flew out.

"Anna! Wait." Diane scrambled to keep up.

"He's going to spray!" Anna was furious. "I told him how I feel and he's going to do it anyway."

"Wait now, think about this."

Anna marched with her arms pumping, fists at

waist height. "I'll have him charged with trespass and willful damage to my property and—"

The tractor was already at the far end of the field. Its headlights swung in a wide arc, making the earth look like a jagged black and yellow moonscape. Then there was a different piercing whine as the sprayer thumped into action.

Anna sprinted down the packed earth at the base of the field, tripped over a clump of earth, and sprawled, cracking her knee on a rock. She quickly picked herself up. Her knee ached, but she ignored the pain and did an awkward run up a row toward the tractor.

"Del VanOrthrum! You traitor!" she yelled, although she knew he couldn't hear her over the noise.

As she neared, she jumped and waved her arms. The glare from the lights left her blinded but she knew Del had seen her by the sound of the sprayer stopping. By the time she reached the tractor, Del had climbed down from the cab.

"How dare you! Clear off my land!"

"Anna! Wait."

He tried to grab her arm, but she flailed at him and stumbled backward. "I'm going to call the police!"

"But it's not—"

"And you dared to call me arrogant!"

"—what you think. It's rotenone."

She suddenly felt small. "What?"

"It's rotenone. It's organic."

"I know it's organic, but where did you get it? I mean, I only have a little tin of the stuff . . ."

"Dad had it."

"Oh," she whimpered. Relief flooded through her. "Oh, Del."

"When I left you, I went home and called him. He told me he had this set aside for our field over here. I was supposed to use it if we got infested with carrot-rust flies, but we didn't."

"I'm sorry I . . . you know . . . I thought . . ."

"Dad said that we might have to do it again in a few days, but that this will stop the hatched insects."

Anna snaked her hands under his arms and around to his back. Her voice was muffled against his cotton shirt. "Thank you, Del."

He hugged her tight. "You'd do the same for me if our situations were reversed."

She would, she knew, but their situations weren't reversed. Anna hated being so needy. He smoothed the hair off her cheek and kissed her forehead. The tenderness made her so weak and soft, tears sprung to her eyes. She just wanted to stand there safe in his arms forever, but Del wouldn't be there forever.

"Want to ride with me?"

"Yes, I do."

Del helped Anna up into the cab. This was smaller than the one she'd been in with him when Ricky got hurt. There was only one seat, a gold-colored upholstery number with a contoured chair and a base that looked like an accordion to cushion his ride. She wiggled down to sit on the floor at his side.

"Comfortable?"

"Very."

Once Del got underway again with the sprayer engaged, he put his hand on Anna's head. She leaned against the warmth of his leg and got settled. They didn't talk much; the engine was too loud. The floor vibrated under her. Every now and again Del did something with his foot that made a muscle in his leg flex under her cheek. It felt intimate and comfortable and . . . right.

Anna twisted to look up at Del, at the way the light from the dash lit up his strong chin. He was smiling. This was the man she loved with all her heart. She had to memorize everything about him because, in a couple of weeks, memories would be all she had left. Perhaps it was just as well. He made her vulnerable. He'd breached the wall she'd carefully built around herself these past few years. It weakened her. If her experience with Chris Parker and his parents taught her anything, it was that the world used up weak people and left walking and talking shells behind.

Chapter Fourteen

Anna slapped her hand on the clock's alarm button and shifted so she half-sat in bed. Her stiff neck and shoulder muscles complained. She longed to snuggle back down in the depression her body had made, but the chickens were waiting for their breakfast and there were still cauliflowers needing wrapper leaves. She dragged herself out of bed and staggered to the curtains. Blood red streaks slashed across the eastern sky. The forecast had called for rain, but it looked as if it would hold off for a while yet.

She pulled on a housecoat and headed downstairs. When the coffee finished dripping, she carried her mug and a bowl of cereal out onto the deck. The wooden chairs glistened with dew so she balanced everything on the railing and stood there with her bare toes curling from the chill.

The sound of chickens clucking and scratching in their runs drifted across the quiet morning air. Anna took a deep breath and was reminded that the chicken coop needed to be mucked out. At least she had the fields almost under control. The cauliflower side looked ragged and unkempt because of the dirt and rotten leaves they'd exposed while working there. The potatoes' side spread like lush, green corduroy. Beyond the rise, the line of hardwood trees looked pale and misty, and in the distance, clouds shrouded North Mountain. A quiet, glorious morning.

Anna had spent the previous day toting a hand-held dusting machine up and down the potato rows, which was why her shoulders and neck felt like rusty joints. It was slow work, going back and forth to refill the canister, crouching and leaning over the plants to get every side of the leaves. Del would be exasperated about it when he heard; he'd asked her to let him use the tractor-drawn sprayer again, but Anna couldn't allow him do things that she was capable of tackling herself.

She finished her morning routine of washing and dressing and tidying up the kitchen, then headed out to start the chores. Most mornings

Anna tried to work around the barn so she could hear if someone came to buy eggs. First, she headed to the road and hung out the colorful *Fresh Organic Eggs* sign.

The chickens acted as if she hadn't fed them in a week. "Okay, girls," she cooed. "Keep it down. You're going to eat out in the run this morning, doesn't that sound like fun?"

They cocked their heads from side to side since they could only watch her with one beady eye at a time, and squawked and complained excitedly. She scooped out a bucket of feed, opened the screen door, and stepped inside the coop. Such excitement! The chickens didn't know whether to run away or flock around her feet. She had to take little mincing steps to avoid crushing one of their gnarled-looking claws. Finally she had a trough dragged out into a run and all the chickens locked out with it. Now she could haul open the wide doors and back a trailer right inside the basement of the barn without fear that the chickens would escape.

Mucking out the chickens was dirty, dusty work. Anna wore baggy overalls, work gloves, a dotted headscarf, safety glasses, and a breathing mask over her nose and mouth. She was in the midst of lifting a fork of soiled chips onto the trailer when a horn sounded. She heaved her load and headed outside.

Karen Smyth, dressed in an immaculate business suit and high heels, stood with her elbow braced on the top of her car. Anna's step faltered. After the scene in the restaurant earlier in the summer, she hadn't expected to ever see the woman in her driveway again. Karen wasn't the type to act contrite, but the very fact that she'd come seemed like apology enough to Anna. Her own animosity toward the woman softened. She decided to act as if nothing had ever happened.

"Hi, Karen. You're up and about early."

"Mother asked me to buy a flat of eggs so she could bake this morning."

"Sure, I'll go get them." Anna finished jamming the work gloves in her dusty overalls. "Unless you'd like to wait five minutes while I collect this morning's? I'll have to wash them."

"I'm too busy to wait."

The basement door was on the driveway side of the house. Anna hurried down to fetch a flat from the refrigerator she kept there. She slid one heavy square off the others and kicked the door closed with her foot. Then she set it on the work table, covered it with an empty tray, and wound twine around the whole thing. As she'd done this so many times before, her hands moved on their own without any thought. She took the invoice book with her when she rejoined Karen.

"Would you settle your account today, please."

"Oh Anna, I don't have time."

"It's $112." That would just about cover the cost of the rotenone she'd used the previous day.

"Just put the flat in the car."

"I don't like my customers' accounts to get too big."

"Oh for heaven's sake." Karen snapped open her purse. "Such a piddle amount. I spend more at my hairdresser's in a month."

No doubt. Karen always seemed to sport a fresh coiffure. Anna tried not to think about how dreadful her own hair must look. The air mask kept the dust from around her nose and mouth, but the rest of her face was filthy. Her headscarf had twisted to one side so it shaded her right eye, and she kept having to bat hair off her left eye.

"If you're going to be honest," Karen continued scornfully, "why don't you just say you're broke."

"All farmers have cash-flow problems this time of year, just before the crops get delivered."

"Farmers," Karen mumbled, pulling out her wallet. "Do you take Visa?"

"Cash or a check."

Heavy sigh. "I hardly ever use cash anymore."

When it looked as if Karen was going to fill in a check, Anna balanced the tray on the car roof to open its back door. She had just bent to lay the flat carefully on the backseat when Karen spoke.

"You've heard about Chris Parker, I suppose?"

Anna straightened so quickly she bumped her skull on the door. "What about him?"

"He's coming home. Bringing a new fiancée."

Once again, Anna marveled at how naive she could be. Here she had been thinking that Karen's appearance was an act of contrition, a mute apology for what she'd said in the restaurant. Not so.

Karen smirked.

Anna refused to be baited. "That's nice."

"You could sue him, you know."

"For what?"

"Breach of promise. He did ask you to marry him, didn't he?"

Anna looked pointedly at the checkbook, but Karen, ignoring her, said, "Do you still have the engagement ring?"

Clearly she knew that Chris' engagement ring had never been returned. Anna wondered if Karen's parents and Chris's were chums? Another thought had her grimacing. What if Karen and Chris's sister, Peggy, kept in touch? No, if that were the case, Karen would have boycotted her long ago. She decided that Karen made the trip all the way to her farm just to tell her that Chris was planning to get married again.

He would want the family's diamond ring back; it had been his grandmother's. Maybe she could get the Parkers to talk to her in exchange for the ring.

"That'll be $112.00," Anna said, keeping her thoughts to herself. "Make the check out to Havenville Farm."

Karen scowled, but she scrawled out the check just the same.

Chapter Fifteen

Anna chewed on a thumb knuckle and stared at the achingly familiar number on the pad next to her phone. When she and Chris were engaged, she could dial that number in her sleep. This time she had to look it up before its combination of deceptively simple digits threw her into emotional chaos.

She turned around and looked at Del's solemn face.

"Go on," he said. "You'll feel so much better once you get this thing cleared up."

"I don't know. Maybe once Chris is married, they'll stop worrying about me."

"Anna, this is a small valley. Your reputation

matters around here, especially if you plan to make a decent living."

"I know you're right."

Del got to his feet. "Would you like me to wait outside?"

She nodded. It did seem harder to do this with an audience. Del kissed her cheek. He looked as if he wanted to say something more, but instead he turned and left the room. A moment later, she heard the kitchen door close.

Finally she took a big breath, stabbed out the number, and listened to three long rings.

"Hello?"

"Mrs. Parker? This is Anna MacFrail. No! Don't hang up!"

"I don't want to talk to you."

"You want the diamond ring back, don't you?"

"Send it by courier."

"You give me ten minutes of you and your husband's time and I'll hand it over."

"Listen, missie—"

"No," Anna snapped. "You listen. I'm coming over in a minute to talk to you."

"I won't open the door."

"Would you rather I waited until Chris and his new girlfriend were there?"

"Don't you dare poison that lovely girl's mind with your lies."

That hurt. There was a time when Marge Parker thought she was a lovely girl. "I'm not telling lies. I've never told lies. Do you want the ring back or not?"

Click. The dial tone hummed in her ear. Anna's heart pounded and her mouth felt dry. The receiver was slick with moisture when she replaced it in the cradle. Maybe she should just courier the ring back? It would be so much easier to do that than to confront the Parkers.

The engagement ring looked smaller than she remembered, and not at all enchanted. She snapped the case closed and put it carefully in a zipped pocket in her shoulder bag. Then she went out on the deck.

The air was balmy and sweet with late summer smells, but Del looked tense, as if he were chilled. He took his hands out of his jean pockets and held his arms wide. Anna slipped into them gratefully.

"Are you sure you don't want me to go with you?"

"Yes, I'm sure, Del. But thank you for offering."

"I could drive you?"

"No, I want to do this myself." She looped

the leather purse's long strap over her head so it crossed her chest.

"What would you like me to do? Wait here? Follow you?"

"No, you go on home. I'll call you tomorrow and let you know how it went."

"Oh, Anna, I feel like I'm letting you face lions all by yourself."

"We're going to have a talk, one we should have had years ago, that's all."

"Oh, sweetie . . ."

"Sticks and stones may break my bones . . ."

Del chuckled and released her. "Please, if you want to talk, or anything. Come over. Or call. Doesn't matter what the time is."

He was so good, so strong, she felt tempted to place herself in his hands. Let him handle the Parkers. Let him look after the farm. Lean on him. Even if he wasn't leaving the next week, she couldn't do that. Her own pride was too important.

Anna wrapped her arms around Del's neck and looked into his eyes. She couldn't mistake the love she read there. Neither of them had ever talked about their feelings. What would be the point? He had his life in Toronto; she had hers here. And then there was the real problem with the Parkers, the one she hadn't told him about.

Anna knew how Del felt about *family*. He believed that families should stick together. He had told her that he would be a raging animal if anyone tried to hurt his niece or nephew. Once he learned how she hurt the Parker family, he would look at her with new eyes, scornful eyes.

No, there was no point in telling him that she loved him.

She waited until Del's truck disappeared down the road before starting her own. It took two tries for the engine to turn over. It was silly of her to feel frightened at all. The Parkers wouldn't hurt her physically. Until this mess, she'd thought of them as paragons of virtue. They went to church every Sunday, didn't smoke or drink. Whenever the grandchildren swore, Don Parker hauled the offender by the elbow to the bathroom for a soapy mouthwash.

She paused on the road and stared up the long paved driveway toward the huge Parker house on the top of the hill. The first time she had seen that house, she thought it looked like a castle, with its four chimneys and thick-glassed bay windows. In the beginning, she let the place envelop her in warmth. It took months to see its seedy underbelly.

A moment after Anna stopped by the house, the kitchen door swung open. Marge and Donald Parker stood there on the top of the cement steps like ramparts blocking her entrance.

"All right," Donald snapped. "Say your piece, give me the ring, and leave."

Anna hugged her purse to her chest. "I want to come inside. I want to sit down and discuss this like adults."

"Oh for pity's sake."

He followed his wife in and let the screen door slam shut. Every muscle in Anna's body was tense as she moved stiffly up the stairs and into the Parker's house. It hadn't changed in five years. Donald and Marge were at the kitchen table looking at one another, their hands in fists on the placemats. Anna slipped onto a third chair.

"First of all, I did not know that you owned that field."

"But you admit to calling the authorities on us."

"Yes, I did make the call. I am so sorry I did that. I honestly thought it was the best thing to do at the time."

Don's face was flushed red in anger. "The best thing for who? You? You were just trying to get back at Chris and you took it out on us."

"I didn't even know Chris was . . ." She paused, swallowed. The fact that their son was about to break it off with her and she hadn't even known had nothing to do with this matter. "I called the Department of Natural Resources because I saw someone using an illegal, dangerous spray and—"

"You're nothing but a snitch!"

"—when I tried to talk to the man using it, he was unreasonable."

Don bellowed, "You should have called us! We could have cleared the whole mess up."

"I didn't know you owned the field."

"You saw who was driving the tractor."

"Yes, Peggy's boyfriend was driving it. But that didn't mean anything. You didn't like the man yourself. How was I to know you hired him? I didn't even know about that property."

"Even so, people don't call the police on their neighbors, not without checking facts. You nearly ruined us. We lost that land. Peggy took the children and moved out west."

"I've regretted making that phone call every day since then. If I'd have known you were involved . . ."

"I don't know why you thought you had the right."

"Did you expect me to just do nothing?"

"That's exactly what you should have done," Donald snapped.

Marge leaned forward menacingly. "We accepted you as part of our family and you betrayed us. Because of you we have no children living within hundreds of miles. We don't even know what our grandbabies look like anymore."

"Your own grandchildren were living in that neighborhood. I thought the spray was danger-ous. Did you want them poisoned?"

"If it was dangerous," Marge said, "Donald wouldn't have bought it."

"But you were convicted . . . ?" Anna didn't finish. Even if she had been wrong about how toxic the spray was, and the Parkers were in-nocent, they still had to pay hefty legal bills.

Donald pushed himself to his feet. "You've had your say. Now give me back my mother's ring and get out of our home!"

"If you'd look at it from my perspective."

The Parkers stood there, looming over Anna, their faces twisted and angry. She let out a shud-dering breath. They'd beaten her again. She fumbled with the buckle on her purse, intending to take out the ring case, but her hand stayed. This was wrong, all wrong. It might be her last chance ever to convince them of her side of the story.

"You don't even have the ring, do you?" Donald said with a low snarl. "You pawned it, didn't you?"

Anna knew if she looked at them she'd lose what little bit of courage she had left. "I made one mistake. I did it with the best intentions. But you two have been slandering me—"

"It's time for you to leave."

Donald pulled on the back of her chair, making her stand up. She marched woodenly toward the door with her heart thudding and bile burning in her throat. The moment she stepped outside, the door slammed behind her. The sharp noise made her start so she missed her footing, teetered on the edge, and fell down the stairs. Anna knelt there on the pavement for three long seconds trying to catch her breath. Then she gathered her purse, made her way to her truck, and drove back down the long driveway under the overhanging branches of elm trees almost defoliated by Dutch elm disease.

Del VanOrthrum stood at the foot of the Parkers' drive waiting for her. His car sat in the pulloff at the edge of an apple orchard.

Anna stopped and wiped her tears off her cheeks with the back of her hands. She rolled down her window and tried to smile. It was very good of him to be there, she knew, but at that moment all she wanted to do was go home, crawl into bed, and stay there.

Del took one look at her face and said, "Shove over."

Chapter Sixteen

Anna tried to snap her safety belt into its slot but her hands were shaking. She was dimly aware that her palms stung. Beside her, Del searched for the lever under his legs to slide the seat further back. Then he cupped the back of Anna's neck in a gently massage.

"I take it that it didn't go well."

She cleared her throat. "A disaster."

He put the truck into drive. "I'm taking you back to my place. It's closer."

"Okay."

"You're so pale. I think you're in shock."

She stared out the passenger window at the darkening fields. There wouldn't be a sunset; the clouds were slate-colored and low.

163

Should she tell Del everything? Why not? He would be gone in a few days anyway. If she told him about her call to the Department of the Environment, he would realize just how trustworthy she was. Oh, he would be gentlemanly about it, but he'd think less of her all the same. Then, once he moved back to Toronto, he'd forget all about her. It would be the best thing. At least if she knew that Del didn't respect her, she wouldn't be waiting around for his calls. She could begin the long process of hardening her heart to pain. Again.

Del guided her into his house and down the hall to a sofa in the den. There he gently wrapped a woven throw around her shoulder, tucking in the ends. Anna's teeth clattered. She pushed off her shoes with her heels and pulled her legs up under the blanket.

"I'm going to get you a shot of brandy."

The thought made her stomach lurch, but she said nothing. Del returned with a brandy snifter containing an inch of the amber liquid. She pulled one hand from the safety of the blanket to take it.

"What the—!" He set the snifter on the coffee table and grabbed her hand. "What happened?"

When he pried her fingers open, she turned her face away.

"I fell."

"Oh, sweetheart. You stay there. I'll get a basin and some warm water." He left.

She leaned over and picked up the brandy. It burned a trail down her throat and made her eyes water, but a moment later she felt braced. The trembling stopped.

"This is ridiculous," she mumbled to herself and threw off the blanket. She wasn't an invalid. This sniffing and hiding under a throw just reeked of self-pity. She didn't deserve pity. She'd made a mistake and she had to own up to it.

"Del," she said when she found him in the kitchen pouring water into a basin. "I want to tell you the whole story of what happened between me and the Parkers. I did do something that caused that family horrible grief. I'm—"

She stopped, startled by the angry look on his face. "What?"

"Your knees."

"I . . . I fell down the steps."

"They pushed you."

"No they didn't."

"Did Donald do it? I'll kill him." His brows drew together and his nostrils opened and closed like a fish gasping for air.

She marched to the sink. "Is this water for me?"

"Anna . . . sweetheart. I can't—I just want to punch something."

The water stung her cuts but she kept her face blank. "When you hear what I did, you'll understand why the Parkers act the way they do."

He stood behind Anna and reached both arms around her. She leaned back into his warmth. Once again, doubts assailed her. How could she tell him? How could she say something to turn him against her? What was honesty, what was self-pride, compared to losing him?

She would lose him either way.

Suddenly she pulled her hands out of the water and turned into his embrace, her damp hands angled away from his shirt.

"Oh Del!"

He clutched her and rocked, as if she were a child needing his comfort and protection. "Anna, I feel so helpless. You've been in love before, but this is the first time for me. I can't stand you being unhappy."

She leaned back and studied his face. Del had just said he loved her. He didn't make a big announcement out of it. It was as if he were so confident of his feelings, and of hers, that it was simply understood.

Anna shook her head. "I've never been in love before. I thought I loved Chris, but now I know I just needed him."

"Oh yeah?" he said, his face brightening. "Here I've been hating the guy and jealous of him all this time, and you didn't even love him."

He set about tending to her scrapes and bruises. His long fingers had grown tanned and calloused over the summer, but they were still gentle.

"Del, would you please make us a pot of coffee? We need to talk."

He smiled briefly, and then frowned. "I have things I want to say to you too, Anna."

She gathered up the papers the bandages had been in, and put them in the recycling bin. By the time she'd rinsed out the basin and dried it, the hearty aroma of coffee filled the kitchen.

Del gently took both of Anna's hands and kissed the palms of each of them in turn. A fissure of pleasure rushed through her. He was so big and strong and handsome, and he loved her! She didn't know whether to cry in anguish or laugh out loud. She couldn't let these feelings distract her, not now.

They made up a tray and carried it back into the den.

"Del," she started.

"Me first," he interrupted.

He lowered himself to one knee. Anna's heart jumped to her throat. A rush of blood thudded in her temples making her giddy and unfocused.

"Anna MacFrail, will you marry me?"

She burst into tears.

Suddenly Del was beside her, rocking and hugging and kissing her hair, her forehead, her tear-stained cheeks.

"I love you, Del! B . . . but I can't marry you."

His body stiffened. "Why?"

"I'm not good enough for you."

He smiled and relaxed. "I'll be the judge of that."

She put both palms on his chest and pushed. "You sit over there. Please, Del, if you're touching me I won't have the strength to do this."

"Okay," he drawled, his face frowning in worry. He moved to an armchair kitty-corner from her.

"The Parkers have good reason to be angry with me. You see, the last time I had dinner there I drove Peggy and her children home. They were living in Woodland then, about a half hour from the Parkers' place. After I dropped them off, I was driving down a short-cut, a dirt road across some fields and wind-breaks. My windows were open and I smelled a chemical. My lips started to burn and . . . I just knew it was noxious. I found an empty barrel of NX-Split-Z."

"Never heard of it."

"It was first used in Mexico, but they banned it decades ago. I learned about it in Agricultural College. It's really awful stuff. I tried to talk to the man using it but he . . . he came at me . . . he scared me."

Del tensed. "Let me get this straight. You were on a dirt road in the middle of nowhere?" She nodded. "And you confronted this guy?"

"I knew him vaguely. It was Peggy's boy-friend."

"Did he hurt you?"

"No. I got in the car and locked the doors. All the way home I kept thinking about what that spray could do to people, about what it could do to Peggy's children. I called the Department of the Environment and reported it. The next day I called Chris, but he wouldn't talk to me. It turns out that the land belonged to the Parkers. They were charged."

"Oh Anna, I'm so sorry."

"So now you know what I did and why they hate me."

"What *you* did? You did the right thing."

"Do you think so?"

"Of course. You couldn't let that stuff get into the air."

"But Del, what if it wasn't NX-Split-Z? What if I read the label wrong?"

"You put it in the hands of the professionals. What else could you do?"

"I should have gone to Donald Parker right away, rather than ratting him out to the authorities."

"But you didn't know he owned the field. And even if you did, you had to stop that spraying right away."

His arguments made sense, but she still heartily wished she'd done anything other than make that call.

"The Parkers were a year going in and out of court. Peggy and her boyfriend left the country. Even Chris left Nova Scotia. So not only did I cause the Parkers to be out financially, I caused their children to move away. Marge said she doesn't even know what her grandchildren look like anymore."

Del scooted back to the sofa. "Do you mean to say that Chris broke up with you because of that? Didn't he understand?"

"He didn't say why he left. I never talked to him again."

"The cad."

"Anyway, now you understand why folks around here don't like me. They use chemicals—not illegal ones like NX-Split-Z—but chemicals. They don't want someone like me snooping around and making farming more difficult."

"I don't believe they'd be suspicious of you if it weren't for Donald Parker. This is all his fault. He shouldn't have been using that junk."

"But you see, that's the crux of the thing. I don't know if he was. I was so sure at the time, but when everything was over, he only got a fine. If he'd been using NX-Split-Z, wouldn't it have been worse for them?"

His chin firmed and he gave it an abrupt nod. "Maybe, we'll see."

She frowned for a moment, not understanding him. He was taking this much better than she had feared, but then he hadn't had time to really think it through.

He drummed his fingers on the arm of the sofa. "How did they find out it was you who made that call?"

"I suspect Peggy's boyfriend told them. And then later I got a subpoena."

He groaned in sympathy. "Did you have to appear in court?"

"No, I sent a lawyer with my deposition."

"Then you don't know what actually went on in that courtroom?" When she shook her head he said, "I think it's time you found out."

Suddenly Del was across the room and had the telephone receiver in his hand. Who was he calling?

"Surely you're not calling the Parkers!"

He shook his head at Anna, but spoke into the phone. "Hi, Sis."

Anna groaned. His sister. The very woman who fought on behalf of the Parkers.

Del continued, "I'm going to put you on speaker phone, Maureen. I'm here with my girlfriend, Anna MacFrail. Anna, this is my sister, Maureen."

"Hello," Anna squeaked.

"Well, hello." Maureen's voice sounded tinny coming through the phone. "Is everything all right? It can't be Dad; I was just talking to him."

"Yeah, I talked to him earlier myself."

"So what do you think about his big news? Can you—?"

"Maureen," Del said, interrupting her, "How do I find out what happened in a court case five years ago?"

There was a long pause before Maureen answered. "The Queen versus Parker court documents are open to the public. You just have to ask for them."

Del frowned at the phone. "How did you know I wanted those ones?"

"It stands to reason." Her voice rose a notch. "Anna? Can you hear me?"

Anna pushed herself off the sofa and stood beside Del. She didn't know whether Maureen was going to lambaste her, or what, but she had to face it. Del took her hand. "Yes, I'm here."

"You did the right thing calling the authorities, Anna. I've always wanted to tell you that, but I represented the Parkers in the action and I couldn't just come out and say it. Once Del checks out those court records and reads them, you will know, beyond a doubt, that you did the right thing."

Anna wept with relief.

Chapter Seventeen

Harvest time in the land of plenty. Anna should have been rejoicing, but her mind seemed to have its own agenda. Three more days and he would be gone.

She swiveled around on the hard seat to make sure the metal blade she dragged behind the tractor was properly lined up in the furrow. She had already dug six rows, so potatoes were scattered across the top of the ground like pale rocks on the red soil. Luckily the sky was overcast. If the potatoes sat in the sun too long they would burn green and she wouldn't be able to sell them.

The two men she'd hired from the Farm Labor Employment Agency busily raked through the dirt and tossed the tubers into canvas bags strapped across their chests. One of them must have filled his bag because he strode over to a bulk bin and upended it. Anna couldn't hear the sound over the rumbling of her old tractor, but she imagined that the potatoes rattled as they bumped onto the wooden floor.

She reached the end of a row and shoved the gears into reverse to back around in line for the next one. Dust kicked up by the blades drifted into her eyes and mouth, but she hardly noticed. Her emotions careened back and forth every time she thought about the previous evening when Del had gotten down on a knee and asked her to marry him. She had said no, she wasn't worthy, and told him why. He had scoffed and said all the right things, but he didn't ask her to marry him again.

What if he did? What would she say? She didn't want to leave this farm; she loved it here in the country. He lived and worked in Toronto, a nice city as far as cities went, but too crowded for her. What would Anna do there?

What would she do here without Del?

She straightened her shoulders. If Del asked her to marry him again, she would say yes. She would sell the farm and, somehow, find a way to pay off her debts. Then she would move into his little apartment in Toronto and devote her time to making him happy. Even the farm, her love for this beautiful farm, seemed insignificant against her love for Del.

If he asked her again.

A movement ahead caught her eye. Del? A shot of joy jolted her into a stand, and then she looked again. Judging by the stiff line of his shoulders and the way he walked up the row with his eyes on the ground at his feet, something was wrong.

She turned off the tractor, grabbed the bar at the side of the cab, and leapt off. The two farm laborers stopped to watch her so she waved them back to work.

She strode down to meet Del. "What is it? Is it your grandmother?"

"No, she's the same."

"What then?"

"I just read the trial transcript." He waved a sheaf of long papers.

She instinctively backed away. "I don't want to read it."

"You don't need to. Just take my word for it, you did the right thing." His lips pressed together angrily.

"I really appreciate you doing this, Del. It takes a tremendous weight off my shoulders."

He still looked preoccupied and angry. "Did

you send that ring back yet?" She shook her head. "Come on then. Let's go return it now."

"I . . . I can't. I have to finish here."

He looked up and down the field. "Tell them to keep picking. We'll probably be back before they're done."

"Del, I don't see any point in subjecting myself to that again."

"I do." He licked his lips. "Chris is back."

Was that why he wanted her to go in person? To prove to himself that she no longer loved Chris Parker? His eyes were stormy with emotion. If it was this important to him, she had to go.

"I'll just tell the men what's up, and then I'll go wash."

"You go wash. I'll talk to them." He took a step away, then stopped and looked back at Anna. "Is that okay with you? You're the boss."

She nodded, but her mouth had dried. Why did he sound so angry? What had she done now? She felt so coiled with tension that she ran down the field to the house.

After scrubbing her face and tidying her ponytail, she grabbed her purse. The diamond ring was still tucked inside. When she got back outside, Del was waiting for her in the truck. She opened the passenger door, but hesitated before climbing up because the court transcript was on the seat like something dirty that she didn't want anywhere near her. Del turned it face down.

She watched him as he drove. A muscle in his cheek appeared and disappeared as he ground his teeth. His knuckles were white on the steering wheel.

A late-model sedan sat in the Parkers' drive. It was probably Chris's rental. Confusion and anxiety made Anna hesitate so she was still sitting the passenger seat when Del came around to her side. He opened the door and gave her his hand.

"It's okay, Sweetheart. I won't let them hurt you ever again."

Relief flooded her. He still looked troubled, angry even, but apparently it wasn't with her. Del wrapped her arm around his.

Chris Parker opened the door. "Anna?"

He looked older and fuller in the middle, but he had the same moon-shaped face and mousy brown hair. "Hello, Chris. This is Del Van-Orthrum."

Chris stepped out on the cement stoop. "Hi. I, ah, remember you from, ah, school. You were a football player."

Del said, "We have a couple of things to deliver to your parents. Okay if we come in?"

Chris looked confused, but he pushed the door wide. Del stepped forward and Anna, still clutching his stiff arm, was propelled along until she found herself back in the Parker house. They followed voices to the kitchen.

"Ah, excuse me?" Chris was valiantly trying to get around Del, to head him off.

They rounded the corner, and all talking stopped. A pleasant-looking young woman stood at the counter with a large, foil-topped bottle of champagne in her hands. When she saw them, she smiled at Chris as if she expected to meet some of his old friends. Marge was there too; her smile froze on her face, making her look like a gargoyle.

Del squeezed Anna's hand, then he left her marooned there alone in the doorway. She felt bereft.

Del pulled the court transcripts from his back pocket and marched over to the table, saying, "I brought you some papers, Donald. Thought you'd want to look them over."

Donald kept glancing back and forth between Del, Chris, and Anna. Then he stopped and glared at Anna, as if he'd made up his mind. She straightened her shoulders and stared right back at him.

Del spread the papers out on the table. The instant Donald realized what he was looking at, he jumped.

"Chris," Del said pointedly, "if you don't

mind, perhaps you'd take your mother and your fiancée—congratulations, by the way—into the living room while we talk about these confidential papers?"

Marge growled as she passed Anna. Clearly she didn't want a scene in front of her future daughter-in-law.

"Chris," Anna said, stopping him.

Chris motioned for his girlfriend to follow his mother through the archway and down the hall. Then he turned to Anna with his eyes downcast.

"This is yours," she said, handing him the velvet box containing the diamond ring.

"Thanks," he said, taking it. "Anna, I'm . . . sorry about . . ."

"I know," she replied briskly.

Chris scurried down the hallway. It seemed amazing that she had thought she loved him. Beside Del, Chris was a weak, boring person.

"Anna?"

Del motioned toward the table, then held a chair for her. He squeezed her shoulder gently before sitting down himself.

"What do you think you're doing, Van-Orthrum?" Donald growled.

"Setting the record straight."

"You've read this?" Donald asked, indicating the court transcript. He looked like he was afraid the papers would bite him.

"I have. Anna hasn't. She's under the mistaken impression that she's responsible for tearing this family apart. Do you want to explain the truth to her?"

Anna could hardly breathe. The mistaken impression? Donald didn't move.

Del continued, "Do you want to tell her how you knew that NX-Split-Z was being sprayed? That you knew and did nothing about it?"

"It really was NX-Split-Z?" Anna cried. "You *were* guilty!"

Donald cleared his throat and said, "I didn't know it was so poisonous. Do you think I would have used it if I did?" His face and neck had mottled red.

"But why . . . why did you say all those mean things to me? Why did you let me believe—?" Anger welled, cutting off her words.

"I thought you'd hurt my son."

"You *thought?*"

"I didn't learn the truth until yesterday."

"How could you put me through that?" Anna whispered. "I was only a teenager myself."

Now the blood drained from Donald's face, but he tried to sound aggressive. "The fact remains, you snitched on us."

Del barked a laugh. "She did the right thing. Weren't you listening in that courtroom? You could have poisoned people."

Donald looked miserable. Suddenly Anna realized that he was an old man. Despite all the pain he had put her through, her stomach clenched in sympathy. They'd done enough now. She started to push her chair back.

Del scooped up the court transcript and crumpled it. "Do you have something to say to Anna, Donald?"

"No," Anna whispered, "he doesn't have to."

Donald said hoarsely, "I guess I've been a bit . . . unreasonable."

Del looked at Anna, questioningly. She gave her head a brisk nod. That was apology enough for her.

Donald rubbed his hand over his mouth, then asked, "Can I offer you a cup of tea?" He looked at the counter. "We were just going to have a drink." He looked uncomfortable again.

"No, thank you Donald," she said, giddy with relief. "We have to be going."

"Another time, maybe," Del agreed. "Right now we've got our own wedding to plan."

Anna grabbed his hand and dragged him from the Parkers' house. They hadn't been there five minutes and already Del had dug her out from under five years of rumor, innuendo, lies, and gossip. They were laughing as they jumped in the truck and swerved down the long drive.

"Oh, Del, you are so wonderful! Thank you."

He scoffed. "I didn't do anything."

She sobered. "You told him we were planning a wedding?"

Rather than turning down the paved road, Del pulled into the orchard and switched off the motor.

"Let's walk."

Fruit hung heavily on the gnarled, low-hanging branches. Another couple of weeks and the blush of red that now colored only on one side would spread around the whole apple. Already the air was pungent with their sweet, tangy scent. Sparrows flitted from tree to tree, chirping happily.

"Anna, a couple of days ago my Dad called my sister and me and made an ... announcement."

She tensed. "Is he okay?"

"Oh yeah. More than okay. The thing is, Dad wants to stay in Holland and look after my grandmother." He smiled. "Maureen and I think he's found an old sweetheart."

"I'm so happy for him." Her voice sounded stilted to her own ears.

"He wants me to run the farm. I said I would do it, only if you agreed to be my wife. Anna, I can't stay in the valley if you don't love me."

She blinked and replayed his words in her head. Then she vaulted herself into his arms.

"Oh Del. I do love you. In fact, I'd already decided to move to Toronto if that's what it took to stay with you. So, if you'd rather we lived there . . ."

"Anna . . . Anna . . . why would I want to live anywhere else than here? We're going to make a success of that organic farm of yours, and we're going to raise a family and— You do want children?"

"I want to have your children."

"Where will we live? Your house or mine? Do you want to get married right away? I do. Dad will come home for the wedding; he already said he would."

"You told your father?"

"He yippeed like a cowboy."

He stopped and cupped her face in his hands. "Tell me what you want, Anna, and we'll do it. In your heart of hearts, what do you want?"

"You, Del. Just you."